Contrition

C. S. SILVERNE

Editing: Hannah G. Wentz at English Proper Editing Services (@englishpropereditingservices)

Cover Artwork: Gentle Veenus (@gentle_veenus)

Interior Formatting: Disturbed Valkyrie Designs (@disturbedvalkyriedesigns)

Playlist

Drunk Enough — Angels Fall
Here Without You — 3 Doors Down
She Hates Me — Puddle of Mudd
Father of Mine — Everclear
Fix Me — 10 Years
If You Only Knew — Shinedown
Glycerine — Bush
Sooner or Later — Breaking Benjamin
Get Out Alive — Three Days Grace
Breaking Inside — Shinedown
Shine — Collective Soul
My Own Prison — Creed
Feels Like Tonight — Daughtry
Cold — Crossfade
It's Been Awhile — Staind
Comedown — Bush
Not Meant to Be — Theory of a Deadman
Second Chance — Shinedown
Far Away — Nickelback

Back to Me — 3 Doors Down
Dear Agony — Breaking Benjamin
Broken — Seether & Amy Lee
Addicted — Saving Abel
Forever — Papa Roach
My Sacrifice — Creed

Twisted Tours is a shared world with Tilly Ridge; however, both novellas in this world are complete standalones and can be read in any order. That said, they will all contain easter eggs from each others' stories to keep the fun alive, and we hope you enjoy them. <3

Translation Guide

1. ***Bésame el trasero***: Kiss my ass.
2. ***Estás pesado y yo estoy cansado***: You're annoying and I'm tired.
3. ***Estúpido***: Stupid
4. ***Hija***: Daughter
5. ***Hijo de puta***: Son of a bitch.
6. ***Ir a pisar una lego***: Go step on a Lego.
7. ***Mamá***: Mom
8. ***Mi Estrella***: My star
9. ***Modales***: Manners
10. ***No hay mierda***: No bullshit / No shit.
11. ***Papá***: Dad
12. ***Por favor***: Please
13. ***Puta***: Bitch / Whore (*strong insult*)
14. ***Sé hacer matemáticas, idiota***: I know how to do math, idiot.

To all of the divorced dad rock lovers who developed nearly their entire personality around rock music—either for the genre... or because some of those musicians are just way too attractive.

Older men will always be superior, and it's even better when they know how to use their fingers accordingly.

Stay emo.

Prologue

ESTRELLA

"Are you ready to go get married, *hija*?" my mother all but proclaimed from behind me. I stared at myself in the mirror and quickly turned my gaze towards hers. Twisting around to face her, my lip wobbled slightly as I noticed tears lining her eyes—yet, I had the sneaking suspicion they were of nothing but joyous belonging, even as her next set of words brought giggles out of my nervous frame. "Like, really? Because we can make a run for it. You know, I almost ran out on your *papá*. I wouldn't judge you in the slightest."

I looked down at the wedges that paired beautifully with the equally white, innocent, and yet untraditional styled tea-length dress that adorned my frame.

Untraditional and unique. *Just like us.*

I was gonna be sick.

"No, *Mamá*. I'm okay. I...just want to throw up a little bit."

"Not on your dress, you won't! All of your pictures

would be horrendous. We have enough pictures of you being sick at those loud concerts. Consider it forbidden on your wedding day."

A chuckle sounded from behind the spitfire of a woman I called my mother, followed by a brooding voice that had haunted me daily for months—nearly as much as Zack's husky one that I would know anywhere. My head snapped up and I tensed marginally as he spoke. "Oh, c'mon, Mrs. Flores. You know you'd have the time of your life at one of those concerts if you came along. We could make you a roadie and everything."

My mother turned to look at me with a raised brow before turning it directly back on Theo. "A 'roadie'? What on Earth is that?"

Theo only continued with a wink. "Oh, they're pretty things like yourself who help out with the... *needs* of musicians on tour. If you catch my drift."

My mouth popped open as I blushed furiously. My mother turned back towards me with a horror-stricken face. "*Hija*! Are you a 'roadie'? Does Zackary know? What are you going to tell him?"

"No, *Mamá*. I am not a roadie," I paused, turning to talk to Theo directly. I glared fiercely as I found him nearly bent over with silent laughter. "And *you* leave my poor, innocent mother alone! She doesn't know any of these terms. You're going to give her heart failure."

Laughter marred his voice as he spoke again. "I know. That's what makes it so funny. I can tell her anything, and she'll think you're a devil. I could absolutely use this to my advantage, you know."

I growled as my mother cut in. "I am standing right here!"

Finally containing his humor, Theo prowled forward. I gulped as he stood directly before me, only to turn, bend down, and place a kiss on my mother's hand. "You are, indeed. And you look absolutely beautiful, if I do say so myself. A band mate would be honored to consider you a roadie."

I really *was gonna be sick.*

It was my mother's turn to blush. "*Oh mi. hija,* are you sure you don't want to marry this brother instead? I think I may like him more."

If my eyes could have rolled to the back of my head, given the horrendous timing and situation that my mother was clueless of, they absolutely would have. My teeth ground down as I responded, "I am absolutely positive."

Theo straightened and turned towards me again. "Ouch."

"Get over yourself."

My mother swatted at my arm. "*Modales.*"

I rubbed the spot on my arm with a pout. "Sorry, *Mamá.*"

Theo smiled sadly as he looked at me, then turned back towards my mother. "Do you mind if I have a minute with your daughter alone? I promise—no roadie behavior. Just a little, private *best man* talk. May as well bash my brother one more time, right?"

My mother, ignoring my all but pleading look, nodded and walked towards the room exit. "Of course! I need to go find her *papá*, anyway. It's almost time, Estrella. Do your last-minute touches!"

And with that, she left me to fend against the wolves. Or—well—wolf.

Dear *God.*

I turned back towards the mirror to hide my nervousness at Theo's close proximity, only to catch my own brown eyes and heavily painted reflection once more. My face held more makeup than I had likely ever worn in my entire life, with my hair being pinned in a cascade of braids and waves that made me appear nearly ethereal.

I was getting married. To my best friend. To my soulmate.

I finally felt the courage to smile at my own reflection as I spoke. Even if it was a tid-bit forced, given how I had loved avoiding the man behind me for three months now. "What's up?"

He stared at my reflection with me, sadness in his gaze, before he said, "I told him."

Dread immediately pulled in my stomach as my head whipped to face him directly. Today was not the day for him to pull a stunt, and if it was the stunt that I thought he pulled, I would be out for blood in the next six seconds. "Who? You told who, *what?*"

"Zack. I told him about that night."

My words came out slow and filled with malice. "What night?"

Six...five...four...

"Oh, you're going to make me spell it out for you? I told him about the night I got shit-faced-drunk and kissed you. And then tried to convince you to leave him for me. Do you feel better now? Should I shout it for all of your guests next?"

And skip a few numbers to one.

I blinked once.

Then twice.

"You're such a fucking *dick*!" The words flew out of me with no caution, and I was unbelievably grateful that my mother wasn't in the room to chastise me. Those were words to have a sandal thrown directly at my head. Even if it was my wedding day.

Theo swallowed roughly. "He deserved to know."

"Oh, fuck you. Is my husband-to-be still here after you told him that one? You know, while our friends and family sit just downstairs, ready to watch us say our *vows*?"

"Of course he is. Do you really think Zack would leave you on your wedding day? I'm the asshole here—not him. But I couldn't let him get married without knowing, anyways. He's still my brother."

"You kissed me!" I nearly shouted the words. "I didn't do anything wrong. *You* made a move on *me*. Do not get it twisted. Do not even phrase it as anything differently. Do not paint me as the bad guy here, like you're 'saving' your brother from being married to a *puta*!"

His blue eyes narrowed into a squint as he crossed his arms. His toned, heavily tattooed arms that bulged way too nicely underneath the black dress-shirt. "I didn't."

That made the alarm bells in my head dim slightly. "You...you didn't?"

"No. I only told him my actions and feelings. You

never told me yours, and therefore I did not place words in your mouth. Though, I would appreciate it if you would stop doing things like gawking at my arms while this conversation, of all topics, is happening. It only makes me want you more, princess."

Princess.

If only murder wasn't a crime punishable for years upon years.

Would a court side in my favor in the case of a man overstepping on a day that was meant to be the best of your life? That should have been in a handbook somewhere.

My words landed with an exasperated chuckle. "I am marrying your brother in ten minutes. Your brother is the love of my life. Zack is my best friend. You were drunk. Maybe you're drunk right now! Whatever the hell it was —is—drop it. Capeesh?"

Theo took one step toward me. And then another one, until he stood directly above me.

I gulped.

He didn't stop there, though. He placed his hands on either side of my head, effectively trapping me against the mirror. I refused to look down or away from him— refused to show him any sign of nervousness—and instead forced our gazes to clash. "I can assure you, princess, that I am not drunk. And I say this with my whole chest now before I probably won't have the chance to do so again. Are you listening?"

I only glared.

The motherfucker had some nerve.

He laughed. "Such a *brat.* Just listen closely, okay? I

am in love with you. I love my brother more than life itself, and I'm filled with nothing but joy over the career we're leading ourselves to, but I would love nothing more than to kick his ass at the altar if it meant I got to keep you for myself. If you were *mine*. I would turn him black and blue for the chance. *Capeesh?*"

A scoff marred my words. "You don't even know me like that, *estúpido*."

"Oh? I don't?"

"No, you don't."

"*Reaallllly?* I think I know just about as much as my darling brother does. The only thing he has a one-up on me is how to make you shiver, squirm, and moan."

A gasp caught in my throat as he lowered his head even more. The sharp point of his nose scraped the side of my neck, and I inhaled deeply at the intimacy, only to be nearly drugged against the woodsy cologne that filled my senses. "This...this is inappropriate. You need to leave."

"One kiss."

"No."

"Estrella." He picked his head up, pleading now, and I watched as his tongue swiped out against his bottom lip. The bottom lip that had nearly consumed me months ago. The bottom lip I had moaned into—because some deranged, fucked up part of me *liked* it. Liked his touch on me. "I will get on my knees and beg for you. One more kiss."

I shook my head. "We can't. I'm not going to hurt Zack like that. He's never hurt me. You were drunk, and I should have shoved you off of me. That's the end of it. No more, no less."

"But what if there is more?"

My heart nearly broke as I had to equally spell out the words for him. I had no idea why rejecting him pained me as much as it did, but it somehow felt like I was closing out a chapter that hadn't even begun. "That won't happen. We won't happen. I've never even told you if I'm interested in you. Zack is my future. Not you."

I watched as his blue eyes went nearly blank at my words, only for him to stand up straight and nod. He looked at me intensely, eyes sweeping from the crown of my head to the French-tip painted toenails in my wedges. He turned swiftly towards the exit, right as my papá entered. "You're a beautiful bride, princess. He's a lucky son-of-a-bitch."

And as my *papá* turned to me with a raised brow, I only shook my head as music began to play.

It was time.

And Theo was right.

Zack would never hurt or embarrass me by leaving me at the altar. But he sure as hell did months later, once I had started believing everything was perfect.

Even with his vow of never letting me go—no matter what.

Chapter 1

ESTRELLA

Every single bone, muscle, tendon, and nerve in my body *ached*, and that didn't even account for the raging migraine tearing through my skull as I shifted my head against the hotel pillow. It only worsened at the sound of some man's voice—Derek, I think—equally groaning against my shoulder blade as his arm tightened around my abdomen. "I need water. And Tylenol. And maybe round five."

Same, same, and absolutely *not*.

I picked my head up from the bed, desperate to grasp the surroundings around us. Except I was met with the sights of an extravagant room, kitchenette, and private pool directly out of the open blinds that only heightened my headache. *Were we in a fucking penthouse?*

Only headliners ever stayed in penthouse suites. And we most-definitely were not in a tour bus.

My head plopped back down on the pillow roughly. "God, how much did we drink last night?"

"Uh...I stopped counting after tequila number six, in

complete honesty. I wouldn't be surprised in the slightest if we polished off a bottle, though."

A groan reverberated out of my chest. "My liver hates me."

"We're in the music scene. We never stood a chance."

Well, he did have a point there. "Let me up. I need to pee. And you feel like a furnace."

His hold released my waist, and I looked down with enough time to see a fully blacked-out tattoo sleeve, paired with the sight of a skeleton hand tattoo, right before he threw the duvet comforter over himself again.

Fuck me.

I wanted to facepalm myself into oblivion. I would know those tattoos anywhere—and not just because photographing them every now and then paid my bills— but also because I actually heavily enjoyed the sound and performance of their music. I had even gone down the YouTube rabbit hole a time or two.

"Did I really just sleep with the lead drummer in Neon Cherry?"

He turned his head to look at me directly before blinking dramatically. "Yeah?"

I groaned. "*Hijo de puta.*"

"Well, that's rude."

My head snapped to face him again as I stood up. I stifled yet another groan, and I was actually surprised that my knees didn't pop considering I must have slept in a near coma-like state. Oh, the joys of getting older. "You know Spanish?"

"Well—no. But I was an immature child who would always Google curse words in foreign languages for my own shits and giggles. I only know *'puta,'* and considering the context, I'm not loving it falling from your mouth."

"Huh."

His green eyes rolled. "Go do your thing so that we can have round five, fireball."

I shook my head as I picked up my discarded clothes on the floor, refusing to feel any sense of shame regarding my nudity. Between the hours of time I somehow managed to carve out at the gym, the thousands of dollars' worth of tattoos that decorated my flesh, and the way this man wanted yet another round—I certainly wasn't going to be shameful at this point. "No can do. I need to start editing these photos, and you need a shower."

"Wow. You really know how to kill the mood. I thought it was fantastic sex that was worthy of more rounds. Why can't the photos wait until tomorrow?"

The more I moved, the more clarity began to flit through me.

Along with my *extensive* to-do list.

God, I really needed Tylenol for the day ahead.

And my goddamned bra.

I shook my head as I finally found it, somehow slung against what probably should've been a dining table of some sorts.

Why did I have the distinct feeling I was the one who was eaten there instead?

"Because you're playing at a music festival in five days, and your social media manager—ya know, the makeup artist who made me look actually hot—wanted these as additional promo. Not that you *need* it, but hey, this is my job. I'm doing what I was hired to do."

"You were already very hot. And I can hire you to do something…"

"Nope. Try again."

"Uh…yeah, okay. I guess you're right. I need to go pick up my daughter from the babysitter. Does that give me any brownie points, though? Single dads are the hot new rager, ya know. Especially when the mom is dead and you're not a deadbeat."

My eyes rolled as I stomped to the bathroom and nearly slammed the door. Though, a smile was somehow on my face at his persistence. It felt good to be *wanted*. Even if…that had to be the weirdest clutch. "I love your music, but I hardly remember last night, and I have bills to pay. My answer is no. Go be a dad, *bicho raro*."

He groaned softly, and I chuckled at how boyish and childlike it sounded. "I don't know that one."

I doubt he meant any harm. But regardless of his intentions—sexual or otherwise—it was me who would still be dealing with at least some form of emotional guilt in the next few minutes, regardless of how well I hid it.

His voice was louder now; I could hear him on the other side of the closed door. "Can I at least get your number?"

My smile dropped.

And there it was.

Shame.

"Sure, yeah!" I shouted back.

It's not like it would go anywhere, though.

Because I was still fucking married to a man that refused to sign divorce papers.

A man that Derek would be playing with at one of the largest music festival events in the United States.

My hands came up to rub my temples furiously.

I needed the *fuck* out of Ohio.

The lyrics from Shinedown's *Daylight* came out of my mouth, mumbled and low, as my fingers played with the photoshop and lighting settings from Neon Cherry's collection. The speaker to my right nearly vibrated with how loud it was. Often, this was the perfect balance for my overstimulated brain while working on a task, but I growled as the neon hues in this particular image refused to balance themselves just right all the same.

The pros of choosing to do professional concert photography were endless. Not only did I get to follow my passion of photography and capturing moments of pure joy, but I also got to travel and befriend some of the best in the industry that had consumed me since I was a teenager.

The cons of choosing to do professional concert photography, however, were navigating the endless varieties of smoke, neon hues, shadows, and shots to capture *the* perfect moment, rather than *a* perfect moment.

It was creativity and science all at once.

And the science was not easy to do when you were hungover and sore as all hell.

My phone buzzed against the soft material of my own hotel room bed, indicating an incoming phone call. I found myself smiling as *Mamá's* name popped up on my screen. Deciding to take a break from the image at hand—featuring a duet song of Colby and Sydnee mid-breakdown—I reached over to simultaneously power off the speaker and answer the phone call.

"Hi, *Mamá*!"

Her voice came through my phone's speaker as I collapsed against the mattress. "*Mi hija*! How are you, baby girl? I can't talk long, but I missed you. I wanted to check on you."

I smiled. "I'm good. You know the drill—work, work, and more work."

"I do. Where are you at now? I call almost weekly and I feel like you're always somewhere different. What... what do they say? You travel as much as a circus? I think that's what they say."

"Maybe. But at least you get to tell everyone that you have a really cool, freelance, alternative daughter. Emo kids are the best kinds of kids, ya know."

"Oh yay. Everything I could have wanted."

"Hey! I thought you were proud of me."

She gasped mockingly now, and I giggled at the ridiculousness of it. "I am! I could not be more proud of you and the name you have made for yourself, *mi amor*. Your *papá* would be so unbelievably proud of you if he knew this is what you had made of yourself after these hard years."

Tears stung my eyes with no warning.

My *papá*.

Fuck, I missed him.

His death anniversary was only a couple short days away, and it explained why I had been working in overdrive lately. I needed the distraction. Because while mourning was never linear, the remembrance that one of your favorite people had left was also crushing.

People always left one way or another, though. I had learned that lesson before him. But it didn't take away any of the ache.

I sniffed and wiped at my eyes as I responded. "Thanks, *Mamá*. I needed to hear that. I'm in Ohio, by the way. I'm sure I'll be heading out in the next day or two. My next assignment is in Texas, and my flight is tomorrow afternoon."

"Ohio?"

"Yeah? Ya know, Midwest land? Where they have a McDonald's and...wheat fields. And that's pretty much it."

"Huh."

I blinked, heavily confused. "What? What's going on?"

"I don't want you to freak out, Estrella."

"Cool, cool, cool. Don't start a sentence like that then. What's wrong?"

"He sent another ticket of some kind to the house. I figured it was trash again, so I didn't tell you. This one was an airplane ticket and a concert ticket of some kind, though. And...it was in Ohio."

Immediately, my face flamed and my hackles raised. My voice was cold and distant when I spoke next. It was always anytime he was brought up with no warning. "When?"

"A month ago."

"A month?! *Mamá*! You should have told me. He still hasn't even sent back the last round of divorce papers back, and it's been two months."

"About that..."

My teeth ground down in anger. "What?"

"There was also a piece of paper mixed in with the tickets. It just said 'No.'"

That time, I really did growl, and I was sure my mother had pulled the phone away from her ear at the sound. I was likely minutes away from blowing a gasket —a trait fallen directly from my *papá*—and I'm sure she would be hanging up any second due to it.

The anger was unbelievably valid though, and I refused for anyone else to tell me differently.

Zack couldn't sign the divorce papers that he should have signed *eight years ago* when he ruined everything and shattered every last innocent piece of my heart—but he *could* send countless tickets and flights to my mother's address for nearly two years now.

Yet, I never found an email, text message, or anything else from him.

A ghost, if not for the random tickets and gifts.

What a fucking joke.

At that exact moment, my laptop pinged with two

notifications. I groaned as I sat up to reach for it. My eyes scanned the emails briefly, though my breath stilled as I held the phone to my ear.

No.

No, no, no, no.

"I have to go, *Mamá*."

"What? What are you goi—" I clicked the red button and tossed my phone half haphazardly. I would end up paying for that later, I knew, but my eyes couldn't help but scan the emails again and again.

To: Estrella Flores

From: Rockin' Wild Talent Agency

Hi, Estrella!

We hope this email finds you well. While we sincerely apologize for this short notice account, one of our photographers assigned to Twisted Tours—anonymous due to privacy stipulations—has been fired from our agency, and we need you to step in their place. Since you are already in the state from our assignment with Neon Cherry, along with your gracious skill level, we thought it would be best to select you for the project. While I do recall you requesting to be taken off this tour months ago, we are slim on last-minute options. That said, with your freelance and open availability contract in mind, we will be redirecting your flight from your current location to one closer to the venue. I am also attaching a set list of the musicians/bands you will be following directly. As a heads up, this list is smaller than general for a week-end-long music festival, due to the high-prolific names, so you will have more free-time than usual. As always, all accommodations are paid for in full. We look forward to hearing from you soon!

Dread filled every part of me as I read the set list next, attached in the form of a PDF with my name, headshot, and information that would be given to every band's media manager, who were all CC'd in the email, as well. My heart beat so fast that I felt the pulse in my ears.

From Stars To Evolution
Neon Cherry
Obsidian Static

Fuck.

There weren't enough curse words in the English or Spanish dialect right then.

I clicked on the second email, and my dread only settled in on itself.

To: Estrella Flores

From: MIDWESTERN AIRLINES

Your flight has been altered and rerouted to the following locations.

Cleveland, Ohio—Harlem, Ohio
    Departing Date: Sunday, March 30th, 2025
    Flight Time: 2:15 p.m.
    Arrival Time: 3:00 p.m.

This flight is a one-way destination.

Baggage, rental car, and hotel accommodations can be found <u>here</u>.

Enjoy your trip!

I stared at my laptop for what felt like hours as I tried to process the information in front of me. My eyes bounced back and forth between the two threads enough times that I was sure I was going to go cross-eyed after so long. Finally, and in an extremely reckless, dumb decision, I moved forward to grab my phone again and texted the only individual I knew was within drinking distance of me.

ME

> Hey. Are you still in town? Do you want to get another round of drinks?

DEREK

> Is this your way of asking for round five?

ME

> This is my way of telling you that I'm about to see my husband for the first time in eight years, and I need tequila. ASAP.

DEREK

Once again, you truly know how to ruin a mood.

Give me thirty. I need to find another babysitter for Maribel.

You have some explaining to do, missy. Text me the address of your hotel.

i'm sorry
But i will always love you. And i'll
come back for you when i'm ready.
Zack

Chapter 3

ZACK

"You have to be *fucking* kidding me," I exclaimed on a panicked breath as I scrolled through the forwarded email that our media producer, Sophie, had sent all of us mere moments ago. "You have *got* to be fucking kidding me."

Theo's head popped out of the bathroom of our shared suite, steam wafting out slowly. "What? Is the Queen coming to the music festival or something?" The top of his hair was wet from his recent shower, buzzed at the sides to show off his skull tattoos, and his jaw was clean shaved. We could have been twins in resemblance—somehow getting our mother's favor in genetics—if it weren't for our facial hair, haircuts, and the slighter, more round curve to my own jawline.

My jaw clicked as I stared at him.

In the last eight years, there were many moments where I wanted to pummel him into the ground. Though, in the last two—once we had finally reached a resolve and resolution—my anger towards him had improved greatly.

Yet, it took seeing her photo on my phone, paired with the knowledge of her arrival, to bring that anger back. And I wanted nothing more than to smash his tattooed head into the glass of our shower doors.

Even if it would land me a few years of jail time.

He took a deep breath as he caught the rage coating my face. It took every ounce of strength to not click my teeth at him next. *Just* to be an asshole. "Okay. Not the Queen. What's going on, man? You haven't looked this pissed off in years. Let alone directed at me. Did something happen?"

I couldn't even find the words as I all but chucked my phone in his direction.

It wasn't like I hadn't seen her in years. I wasn't shocked to see her beautiful face, nor her split colored hair or golden complexion. I had stalked my wife more than any fan could have ever stalked anyone in our band—watching her age, change hair colors, get more tattoos, and experience life. I often fell asleep in my bed, a hotel bed, or a tour bus staring at her. Her photos.

At her happiness.

At her happiness *without me.*

No, I wasn't shocked to see her in the slightest. What I was shocked to see, however, was that she would be working for us—involuntarily—when I had been begging and pleading to see her for just over two years. Text messages, letters, and countless tickets had gone unanswered.

Even when the divorce papers were still being delivered.

Only for her to show up anyway. *For her job.*

An ache pounded at my heart at the realization.

She was only coming because she had to for her livelihood.

Not for me. Not for *us.*

Theo's whistle brought me back down to reality, and I rubbed my anxious palms together as he spoke. My anger was slowly beginning to fade into absolute terror. "Damn. That's our girl. She's working for us? I didn't know she had responded to anything you sent," Theo commented.

I nearly growled. "She *hasn't.* And she wasn't supposed to be working for us, either. The email says our previous photographer was fired due to a deadline issue or some shit. She's being sent to us against her will."

"Oof."

"Fucking *oof?* That's what you have to say right now, you jackass?"

"Uhhhm," he started, scratching at the nape of his neck. "But like, she's still coming, right? There's a positive side to this. We can actually talk to her. We can explain ourselves. This is a good thing, man!"

I blinked before my head dropped to my tattooed hands. I couldn't tell if I wanted to laugh, scream, or cry. The emotional intelligence that came with heartache, longing, and loneliness often turned you into a brittle shell of a person, and yet, I somehow only felt the highest of highs or the lowest of lows—all at the same exact time. "She's never going to hear us out."

"Yes, she will."

"No, she won't."

Theo kicked at my black Converse, and I jumped back in shock. I didn't even hear the fucker walk toward me. Yet, there he stood, towering over my pathetic, weakened frame—shirtless, wearing just a pair of black boxers, and showing off all of his tattooed ink. Too close for comfort without a buffer. "You left the love of your life because I was a jealous dumbass who made you choose between love and blood, and yet you've stayed faithful to her for years, even when you could've just moved on. You never forgot about her. For fuck's sake—half of our songs and our hidden album are *about her*. She just...needs to give us one more shot. And we can go from there. She'll hear us out."

I gnawed on my bottom lip.

Easier said than done. Especially from Mr. Sunshine over there.

"Yeah...right. Because not only do we have to explain to her why I broke her heart and you deserted her as her friend and brother-in-law, but we also have to explain the following sentence: 'Hi, my star. I've missed you. Theo and I have talked some over the last eight years, ya know, and we want to share you. Together. Forever. Yay us. What do ya say?'" I took a deep breath before muttering, "Fan-fucking-tastic."

"Well...I probably wouldn't phrase it like *that*. That wouldn't be very tumblr-happy, polyamory of us in those terms."

"Fuck you."

"That's incest."

"I want to beat you into the ground until you're nothing but a pile of mush."

Theo ignored the jab with a shrug and continued. "Listen. You can change your mind, you know? I can move on. I've seen you torture yourself for years. That girl is your soulmate, and I'm the intruder here. If you want to go back on what we talked about...I can get over myself, somehow. I may be in love with your wife, right alongside you, but I think I've put you both through enough hell. Don't you?"

My answer was immediate. "Yes. Yes, you have."

His blue eyes nearly rolled to the back of his head in annoyance. "Gee, thanks. Here I was trying to make you feel better."

My resounding sigh could have echoed throughout the suite as my eyes bounced around manically. Except, when they landed on my own flesh, it was the tattoos on my left hand and forearm that only solidified what I knew. I traced them absentmindedly as I thought about my next words to Theo.

An abstract sun on my forearm.

A star on my left hand's ring finger.

And a blazing lightning bolt connecting them both.

My sunshine filled brother and my star of a soulmate —tethered together from the destruction of lightning labeled as myself.

I could never let either of them go.

And Theo was full of shit for even suggesting he could let her go.

She was ours. She was our evolution.

Estrella had consumed us both for so long, even

when we were immature and wanted to play tug-a-war with her soul, that she literally became the name of our entire career.

From Stars to Evolution.

I knew better than to think he would ever let her go. Especially after so many years and shared conversations. If she even gave me a chance, yet ignored him—he would be in pain for the rest of his life.

While I had considered my star as my soulmate...it took nearly a decade to discover that maybe a soul could belong to two people and still be happy—if she could allow herself that pleasure and contentment, too.

As I met the eyes of my younger brother, I questioned how life had to be so ironic and yet torturous. His eyebrows were pinched in worry as he stared back at me, likely already accepting the rejection that would never come, and my head ached as the words flew out of my mouth with no hesitation. "Hurting her was the biggest mistake of my life. I'm not going to hurt her again. And for what I've put her through—what we've both gone through—she deserves love from us both, if she'll even accept it. So, if I have to share her with anyone—it'll be you, brother. We all deserve a chance to be happy now."

His shoulders sagged in relief.

Yeah, I still wanted to punch him. Regardless of how true my words were.

I continued as I stood up. "You're the one who has to explain everything to Sophie and the guys, though. Starting from the beginning. I'm not going to be the one to tell them that our entire persona is pretty much built over the love of my life that *you* made me toss away. And that we both have to beg for."

"Okay, yeah, that's fair. Yes, sir." His eyes followed me as I grabbed my wallet from the table and headed for one of the private bedrooms that housed our band. Our band, that somehow, knew absolutely nothing about any of this damn mess. It was a damned miracle. "Where are you going?"

I slammed the door behind me as I spoke. "I've been celibate for eight damn years, and my wife will be here in twenty-four hours. I'm jerking off until my balls turn into raisins so I don't bust in my jeans just at the sight of her."

His resounding laugh was loud as fuck. "Hey, I've been celibate for two years, too. You think I should do the same?"

I ignored him as I laid down in bed.

I had no intention of touching myself, in all actuality. I didn't give a fuck if that even did happen.

Instead, I was going to scroll through social media and photo galleries to stare at my star in peace.

And also pray she would give me—give us—one last shot. One chance to prove to her that we were both profoundly sorry, but that we would also do anything to keep her.

Even if I had to grovel like hell.

700
52x
80
CD-R
disc

Chapter 4
THEO

"Alright, boys!" I clapped my hand as I met the eyes of everyone in our band. They landed on Zack first, and I watched as he anxiously scanned the tents of arriving assistants, photographers, and fellow musicians that had yet to check in—likely searching for her, even when we didn't know when exactly she would arrive. Shaking my head, I tore my gaze away from him and landed on Elijah, Alex, and Tyler instead. At least they would be focused enough for a little speech. Even if the back of my neck prickled with how badly I wanted to join Zack in his anxious searching, too. "As you all know, we're a headliner for Saturday night. Generally, we stick to a specific set list for festivals. But I wanted to let you all know that we will likely be adding a song from our unreleased album into the mix now as a teaser. Are you all confident with that? Or do we need to have some practice rounds?"

Tyler was the first one to throw a barb. "You do know

it's Thursday afternoon, right? Why are we worrying about Saturday night?"

Elijah answered that one for me. "Because we're pros, you dumbass. He needs to know if we need a soundcheck or rehearsal before we're in front of thousands of people."

Alex spoke next as he tapped his drumsticks against his own thighs. The guy was always trying to find new melodies to pair with future lyrics. "You mean the album about—"

"Shut up," I interrupted, clapping firmly. My smile had malice in it as I stared at him. He meant no harm in asking any question, but I had no idea when Estrella would arrive—if she would even arrive today—and I absolutely did not need her to overhear what or *who* our unreleased album was about. Especially after the lovely chat I had with everyone mere hours ago. "Yes, that's the one."

Alex rolled his eyes into a squint as he spoke next. "Alright. Morse code it is, I guess. We've played those songs dozens of times. Probably more than needed for any rehearsal. I think we'll be just fine."

Finally, Zack spoke, and I nearly sighed in relief that the pressure was being taken off me. Even if I was somehow the happiest and most optimistic person in the damn band—I was still freaking out on the inside, too. This weekend could literally make or break our entire existence, and the only person who understood that was Zack. Having everyone's eyes on me didn't help that in the slightest. "We'll still probably practice the day-of. Theo and I are going back and forth on which two we want to play, though, but we'll let you guys know as soon as possible. That cool?"

The group only responded with a resounding chorus of "yes," "yeah," and "sure."

Start a band with the grumpy emo kids you met in college, they said. *It'll be fun,* they said.

Well, it was pretty fun, in all actuality. But man, did their communication suck.

"Beautiful," I responded as I rubbed the back of my neck and walked closer to Zack. The scent of fresh cut grass filled the afternoon air, and while I would generally act like a golden retriever with a frisbee over the warm air, I could have sworn that the prickle of awareness had only gotten stronger. I looked down at my watch to check the time as I reached his side. "If that's the case, then I guess we're free to roam. Just don't stay drunk the entire weekend. And if you do—for fuck's sake —*stay* drunk or have an assistant go pick up some Pedialyte, because we cannot afford the hangover at this one."

"We're literally sharing a hotel suite. I think we'll be checking in on each other more than you think," Tyler scoffed.

It was my turn to eyes to roll obnoxiously. *Fucking liar.* "Like you boys won't be buried in pussy the whole time. Stay out of the suite with that shit. Some of us are good, behaved men who don't want to hear your pornos."

"Awe, what if I wanted to have live action porno? That sounds like a fun time." My head snapped up and to the right as a female spoke, and I felt Zack immediately tense right alongside me at the sound of her voice. "I could call you a good boy if it makes you feel better."

Estrella.

Estrella...and...*a wiener dog?*

"Estrella," I said. It was literally the only word that entered my head, and it bounced around like a ping-pong ball. She stood mere feet away from us, carrying the sausage-like animal, though had yet to even look at us as she signed a check-in slip. She grabbed the staff lanyard and a black wristband with green accents from the assistant in front of her.

Fuck. She was beautiful.

Her hair, split in half with black and neon green color blocking, twisted itself into braided space buns. She wasn't wearing any makeup—like she even needed it—and wore the simplest outfit of an oversized t-shirt, tucked into her bra to show off her midriff, and skin-tight, black short-shorts.

And...tattoos. So many tattoos. Light florals and butterflies on her arms, paired with heavy ink of skulls, quotes, and lyrics all along her opposite leg.

Like beauty and chaos, all in one.

Granted, I had seen pictures of them *and* her, but they did her no justice. Not in person.

Don't get a boner, don't get a boner, don't get a boner, I chanted to myself. *She hates you and will cut off your dick.*

Her tone held all the sarcasm as she finally looked at me, ignoring everyone else entirely. Including Zack. "That is my name, yes. I'm glad to see you've remembered it after so many years. *Good boy.*"

My jaw ground down as Alex barked out a laugh. "Oh, I like this one."

Estrella smiled at him as she looped the lanyard around her neck. An intense strike of jealousy lit down my spine, seeing her smile directed at someone else. That and knowing her moment of praise was more brat and humiliation than anything. "Thanks! I dig the hand tattoos. I bet you give the prettiest hand necklaces."

I could have sworn Alex nearly blushed. His voice contained his swagger as he continued, though. "We can always test that out, ya know."

Zack spoke next, and I was actually surprised at how firm and possessive he sounded. "Paws off, mother-fucker. Go find another one to test that theory on."

"Lame…" Alex muttered.

Estrella only chuckled before she pet the head of the wiener dog. It whined in her arms, scratching at her to be let down, but she only cooed at it as if it was a baby. "C'mon, Mildred. Just a few more minutes. We got this. It's just some gross, testosterone-filled men. Your daddy will be back soon."

…Daddy?

I finally found the courage to speak again. "You look…good." I swallowed roughly.

"That sounded confident. Great flirting, asshat," Alex mocked me.

"Ah, don't worry about it. They haven't seen me in eight years. Ya know, walking away from a whole life and shit. I'm surprised he's even found his words," Estrella said before nudging her head in Zack's direction. "He's yet to say much though. That—well, that I certainly expected, given his communication over the last decade."

Somehow, simultaneously, Tyler, Alex, *and* Elijah whistled at the exact same time.

The fuckers.

Elijah spoke next. "Holy shit. You're…"

"Estrella Flores. Casual drinker, intense fighter, your photographer for the weekend, his wife, and his sister-in-law. It's a pleasure to meet you three. We'll need to talk soon about your set list, any specific requests for your social media, and more. Is Sophie around? Do you three have time in the next few hours or so? Before the chaos of the festival really begins?"

"Uh…yeah, sure," Tyler spoke. It looked like he nearly wanted to scratch his head in confusion. "You don't seem spooked out in the slightest, ya know. I'd be shitting bricks if I were in your place right now."

"What do you mean?"

"Working with us. Ya know. Given all your personal history and whatnot. You seem like this is just another typical Thursday. And you're very organized."

Estrella looked me directly in the eyes first before they landed on Zack's heavy gaze. Regardless of the cool tone she held, I saw the hidden emotions floating around —and they contained utmost agony and livid anger. My heart nearly broke at the sight. "Ah, well…when someone you called *the love of your life* walks out on you with no warning—it definitely turns you into a different person. But I've learned and accepted that I don't owe these *burros* anything. I'm here to work, and you all deserve the best."

Alex spoke next. "So...you are on the table then?"

Estrella snorted as I nearly saw red. My head whipped in his direction. I was going to catch murder charges soon. "Nah. You're very cute, but I'm running away from this band the second this tour is over. I do appreciate the compliment, though."

Zack finally fucking spoke to her as words clawed at my throat, too. "Estrella, can we talk? Please?"

Another male's voice sounded over the chaos, and my eyebrows bunched together in confusion. Was she dating someone? Did she bring a boyfriend of sorts with her? And their *dog?*

Was that the supposed...Daddy of Mildred?

"Estrella! Mildred!"

"Over here!" Estrella responded as she turned away and waved her hand at a man who wore a full-beat face of makeup, complete with a set of false lashes and pink lipstick. He huffed out a sigh of relief.

Okay, what the fuck?

"Oh, come to Daddy," the man said as he took the wiener dog—Mildred—away from her. "Thanks for watching her, girl. There are so many gothic weirdos around her. I was terrified someone would step on her with studded boots or something."

"Oh, it's no problem. She's goofy. I'll babysit your baby anytime."

"Estrella!" Zack cut in, his voice deep and hard as stone. Estrella jumped and faced him, and I nearly flinched from the sound of it myself. "I need to talk to you."

I watched as her eyes rolled and she propped out a

hip in annoyance. "No. You, of all people, do not get to demand anything from me. Are we clear? We will talk when I want to fucking talk to you. *If* I ever want to talk to you again. Got it?"

Zack only stared at her.

My eyes bounced between the two of them.

She shook her head at his silence and scoffed before walking away.

Elijah spoke next. "Oh, you guys are *fuuuuucked.*"

And then Tyler made eye contact with the man in front of us all who held the sausage-roll-animal. "Who brings a wiener dog to a music festival, bro?"

The man sniffed as he followed Estrella. I could have sworn he even walked in a preppy style. He threw words over his shoulder. "I will have you know, Mildred is more of a badass than you fuckers will ever be."

And as I met Zack's face—I, too, realized we were fucked indeed.

"What a fucking dick!" Derek said as he threw back his own shot of tequila. I handed him a lime slice to suckle on with a giggle as he continued with a pinched brow. "You know, I've met some cowards in my life, but that's a whole new level. Not only did he abandon you, but now he thinks that he can talk to you like that, too? That's crazy."

"Isn't it?" I exclaimed. I was intensely buzzed as I rambled Derek's ear off—yet again. And while this would generally be a dangerous combination considering I had liked this man enough to have sex with him in the same setting mere days ago...I didn't even care.

Fucking Zack thinking I would drop everything to talk to him the second I saw him.

Fucking Theo thinking he could compliment me and I would bat my eyelashes like a love-sick school girl.

Fucking *me* for feeling heartbroken as soon as I walked away.

The only men safe from my wrath were the other shitheads in that damn band, and even then, I probably wouldn't protect them if some weirdo came at their million dollar hands with a baseball bat. Simply because they were connected to the men who ruined me.

Survive the weekend, I told myself. *Survive the weekend and then you can run away.*

I continued even as my words had the faintest hint of a drunken slur. Had I eaten anything that day? I couldn't even remember. That probably wasn't a good sign. "And you know, maybe I will hear them out. Maybe I'll even try to see if there's anything that can be repaired. But I will do that on my goddamned terms! They don't get to boss me around as if I am that young, naïve, twenty-one-year-old girl anymore."

Derek's eyes pinched together with a questioning head tilt. "Would you take him back? Or take *them* back into your life at all?"

I plopped my elbows up on the bar top before dropping my head in my hands. "I don't know. I came here thinking I would throw the—yet again—rejected divorce papers in his face. I've been over him for years. I wouldn't have slept with you or anyone else if I thought we had a chance ever again. And then...one look at the men that I used to call my best friends had me in more pain than I've been in years."

"That's not good."

"*No hay mierda,* Sherlock."

"Hey! You texted me. No cursing at me in your fancy... really sexy tongue. I'm trying to be a friend, and that only turns me on. So shut up. I'd rather not think about fucking your face while you're crying over your piece-of-shit husband and brother-in-law."

I groaned.

"Well, doesn't this look cozy," a voice I would know anywhere said as a heavy arm was thrown over my shoulder. "Excuse me if I misunderstood or anything, but did you just talk about fucking her face?"

My shoulders grew impossibly tense at the drop of a hat. I looked up in a daze to confirm my already-known assumption. "Theo."

His blue eyes flew to mine, and I flinched at the anger that they held. Somehow, they softened when he saw my reaction. "How much have you had to drink, princess?"

Derek spoke for me. "She's had a lot."

"And that's your doing?" Theo asked, his eyebrow raising in fury as he turned back towards my...*friend?* Could you be considered friends with someone who gave you really strong orgasms?

"Me? No. There's no controlling that fireball of a woman. But I have matched every single one of her shots. If I'm buzzed, I don't even know how she's going to stand."

Theo sighed as his gaze turned back toward mine. "This is my fault, isn't it?"

I laughed. It almost sounded like the Joker had possessed me at that moment. I spoke as I tried to shrug him off me. "Yes. Yes, it is. I'm so glad you could come to that realization yourself. Now, get your arm off me. *Estás pesado y yo estoy cansado.*"

"Did you just call me fat?"

A very unladylike snort flew out of my mouth. "Maybe."

"Alright." Theo sighed as he pulled the barstool away from the tabletop. I squealed as his arms wrapped around me, with one arm going underneath my knees and the other going under my arms, before he lifted me effortlessly. "Time to get in bed. C'mon."

"Let me go, you mongrel!"

Derek stood up abruptly before he was directly in Theo's face.

In my face.

I gulped at the testosterone that surrounded me, all in the blink of an eye. God, I really was blasted.

"Hey, hey, hey. Listen, I don't care if you're her brother-in-law or not—not after what she's told me. If she doesn't want to go with you, then she's not going anywhere. So, either sit the fuck down with us until she makes up her mind, or you're gonna have to go through me first. Don't make me kick your ass because I will."

Theo took in a deep breath before he looked down at me. "Will you please go with me?"

A part of me wanted to spit in his face.

The other part of me just wanted to burst out in a fit of drunken tears.

Fuck, life was unfair that week.

"Are you going to hurt me again?"

"*What?*" Derek exclaimed loudly. I was so unbelievably grateful that this round of hotel staff had been warned about loud men coming to their premises, because when I looked up, people around us were well and truly minding their own business. It was normal for musicians to be ruefully loud. "He's hurt you? What the fuck, man? Put her down!"

I shook my head as I leaned to rest my head against Theo's chest. He certainly wasn't my first choice as a pillow, but I was running short on options. "Not...not like that."

Theo ignored Derek. I had a feeling he was mere moments away from losing his shit entirely. "Princess, I will get on my knees and beg. Will you please let me take care of you tonight? You can go back to hating my existence in the morning, okay? I'm not letting you be alone anymore tonight, though. Alcohol is only making everything worse."

I huffed as I nuzzled closer to him.

The prick was warm, and it was as agitating as it was comforting.

"Fine."

Derek sighed, and I watched as his fingers raked through his hair in stress. "Are you sure, Estrella? You can stay with me if you prefer."

Theo's snarky comeback was quick as he walked away. "Oh, so you can think of face fucking her some more? Fuck you. I'm taking my girl back to our own suite. I don't know what past you two have, but it ends here."

His footsteps were heavy as he carried me throughout the hotel. I had the faintest feeling that people were watching—probably even pointing and whispering—but I didn't have it in me to care.

I wanted to lay in bed. And I wanted to cry. Humiliation and shame had begun to mix in with my buzz the second that Theo picked me up, and it was only growing.

What has my life become?

As Theo stepped into the elevator, somehow managing to press the button to his floor, tears leaked down my face without my control. I sniffled as my shoulders shook along with them.

Fuck, I was crashing.

I pulled back to look Theo directly in the face with words that I knew would hurt him. I had to hurt him in some way to level the pain they had both caused me. *Somehow.* I hoped that the tears on my face would be more convincing than not. "I'm not your girl."

He didn't even flinch as he looked back at me. "No. You're ours."

"What?"

The elevator dinged as the doors opened, and I watched as we stepped out of it and directly into his private, penthouse suite.

Of-fucking-course.

They were headliners. Just like Derek's band. Richer than rich.

Zack stood by the elevator doors anxiously, and my tearful eyes met his sad, red-rimmed irises.

I flinched.

Why was *he* crying?

Theo hardly paid him any mind. Instead, he carried me past him, and only shook his head as he walked me into one of the bedrooms. As if he knew I couldn't handle talking to him yet. Though, his next set of words confused me more than anything—and I didn't know if I could blame the alcohol that time. "Introduce me as your brother-in-law to anyone ever again, and you will be bent over my knee and punished accordingly. Are we clear?"

As he laid me down in bed, still in my outfit and lanyard from the day previously. I shook my head in a mixture of confusion and annoyance.

I couldn't even muster a reply as sleep hit me mere seconds later.

i'm sorry
but i will always love you. And i'll
come back for you when i'm ready.
                                        Zack

Chapter 6

ZACK

I laid on the couch, twisting and turning for hours at the sounds of the thunderstorm that had begun nearly as soon as Estrella passed out—all while she slept in my bed, mere feet away from me—praying she wouldn't wake up to it. Theo had tried to convince me to sleep in his room with him, but I had refused, claiming that I didn't want to give her the chance to sneak out later.

That wasn't the entire truth, though.

The real reason why I wouldn't get into his bed was because Estrella had always been afraid of thunderstorms, and I doubted that fear had gone away in the last decade. Not when they used to make her have panic attacks as a child. And I couldn't bear the thought of her freaking out alone, should she do so.

It was one reason I sent Theo down to retrieve her when I walked past the bar and saw her shots deep already. The forecast had pinged a warning on my phone, and anxiety filled me instantly.

Not for me, though.

But for her.

So, a lumpy couch to hold for my already-aching, forty-two-year-old body it was.

I'd be paying for it the next day.

Fuck, I'd be paying for a lot of my life decisions the next day.

I was unbelievably thankful that we didn't perform that next night, or else thousands of people would have undoubtedly witnessed me with as much makeup on as the wiener-dog owner wore for my under eye circles alone.

Which...nothing against him. It actually looked really good. That was a talent.

I'd have to pass on it myself, though.

My body tensed as a crack louder than hell sounded throughout the air, followed by a blazing lightning bolt that showed itself through the sheer curtains mere moments later.

And then another crack, even louder, in its wake.

Fuck.

I held my breath and counted.

One...two...three...four...

Crack.

Five...si—

The door to my suite cracked open and I watched as a pale Estrella walked out into the space, shivering and holding both of her arms tightly, almost as if she were hugging herself. She looked like she had seen a ghost, and my gaze raked over her as she tiptoed out further.

She had untucked her t-shirt from her bra, and it nearly went to her thighs.

God, she was beautiful.

I doubted she had noticed me watching her, considering I was mostly covered by a thick, black duvet blanket from Elijah's room—who had never come back to the suite, along with any of the other guys. Convenient, but I merely shrugged and took advantage of my situation.

Deciding to try not to scare her should she get closer to me, I called out to her. "Over here."

I sighed as she jumped anyway.

Though, her head was pointed right at my direction, indicating she knew exactly where I was.

Nice going, dumbass.

She stood stock-still as she stared at me. "Zack?"

"Yeah, baby girl," I replied, wincing at the ease of how the pet name came out. I was supposed to be handling this with care, and yet my tongue had me jumping into the snake pit immediately. "You wanna join me?"

"Are...Do you have clothes on?"

That's what she was asking?

"Uhm. Yes? Why?"

"I wasn't going to get near you if you were naked."

"You act like you haven't seen me naked before. Or that we aren't married."

Her arms only tightened around her at that, and my heart panged as I heard her sniff. She was crying again. *Fuck me,* I was an absolutely damned idiot. "That's so not fair."

"What's not fair?"

"You. This. That. You don't get to say that to me right now. That's not fair."

I hung my head. "You're right. I'm sorry. I...we have a lot to talk about. Can you just come here, please? I know you're freaking out right now, and it's absolutely killing me."

Another sniff—though this one was followed by a large flinch as yet another crack filled the air. As lightning hit the surface of the sky, my eyes got a better glimpse of her face in the dark. It wasn't much, but it was enough to see her lip wobbling and tear-stricken face. "Why?" she asked.

"Why what, love?"

"Why is it killing you? Why do you even care? Why now? Is this just a game to you?"

I sighed before giving her a mere fragment of the ache that surrounded me. "No, Estrella. You were, and have never been, a game to me. I've never stopped caring about you. I've never stopped loving you. Now, would you get underneath these blankets with me so I can hold you through the storm? We can talk about everything more tomorrow."

She stared at me, debating.

The seconds felt like hours as she weighed her options.

If she went back into the room by herself, I wouldn't follow her. I'd give her the peace she deserved. The processing time she needed. And yet, I couldn't help but release the breath I didn't even realize I was holding as she walked towards me, flung the duvet off of me, collapsed on the couch, and then threw the blanket over us once more. Clinging to me.

"Fuck, baby," I groaned. My arm wrapped around her waist and I tugged her closer to me with her back at my chest. "You're shaking like a leaf."

"You don't get to call me pet names."

I flinched like she had smacked me, grateful she couldn't see my facial reaction to that statement. That was more than deserved, though. "You're right. I'm sorry."

She huffed, even as she wiggled impossibly closer to me. I bit my lip as her ass nearly ground into my dick, but forced myself to remain calm and neutral. "Don't do that, either."

"Do what?"

"Make me want to forgive you just because you're being nice to me."

"I-I'm sorry?"

"Stop it!"

I shook my head even as my grip on her tightened. "I really don't know what you want me to say or do right now, Estrella. I just want to be here for you right now. Tell me what I can do."

Another thunder crack filled the air, but that time, she flinched into me rather than by herself.

Even knowing she felt safe enough to cower into me felt like being placed on a pedestal.

I'm so sorry, baby, my subconscious whispered. *Let me take care of you.*

Her voice cracked in half as she spoke seconds later. "Why did you leave me? Why are you being so nice to me now if you cared about me all along? What the *fuck* is happening?"

I tucked my head into the crook of her neck and inhaled. My heart shattered at the sound of her voice and the scent of her. The scent and warmth I had missed more than anything over the years. "Tomorrow. Let me tell you everything tomorrow. Then you can decide if you hate me. Okay?"

Her shoulders shook as the tears kept coming. "You've hurt me so bad."

"I know."

"I shouldn't forgive you. Ever."

"I know."

"But I want to."

God, I felt like I was being nailed into the ground. I deserved every single hit, though. My own voice cracked as I spoke next. "I hope you do."

Seconds passed. I could have sworn that I even dozed off as the silence wore into minutes—maybe even hours. Her warmth surrounded me, and though her trembling never stopped, it did lessen from genuine fear and more into anxious thrumming. Though, I was somehow wide awake in a second when she spoke next. "Zack?"

"Yeah?"

"I'll always love you, too."

My mind flew to the memory immediately. The absolute coward and lame ass note I had left her when...when I left us.

I'M SORRY

BUT I WILL ALWAYS LOVE YOU. AND I'LL COME BACK FOR YOU WHEN I'M READY.

ZACK

"I meant it," I whispered as I tucked my mouth into her hair. Kissing the crown of her head. "I'm just so sorry I didn't come back soon enough."

"Yeah. You were too late for a lot of things."

And like fate, another thunderstorm crack sounded —right as I felt a crack split down the center of my chest. I don't know what all I had missed exactly, but I would find out, one way or another. She jumped as lightning flit through the room again, though I only held her close and kept my lips in her hair. My mind raced as I thought about what I could possibly do to take her mind off of the raging storm. Until...

"Estrella?"

"Hmm?"

"You remember what I used to do when we were biding time for the thunderstorms to calm down? All those years ago?"

She tensed in my arms. "Oh, fuck you."

I chuckled. "Hey. I know you hate me and all, but you're still right here. Right in my arms. Right where I need you to be. You can't blame a guy for thinking about the past."

"You're thinking about finger-fucking me to take my mind off of a thunderstorm...when we were literally just talking about how you shattered my heart and irrevocably changed me."

My fingers twitched against her side. I loved when she called me out on my shit. It's what made me and Theo fall in love with her. One of the things, anyway. "Yeah. And eating you out. And I'm thinking about how good you taste, and how badly I wish I could make you shake in a different way right now."

"You're not playing fair in the slightest," she groaned. I had the faintest suspicion she'd be blushing if I could see her face in the dark.

"I'm just talking. I never said I was a saint."

"*Bésame el trasero.*"

I barked out a laugh. "That's what I want to do, yes."

"Y-You learned Spanish?"

"We both did. Theo and I. It's a part of you, so it's a part of us, too."

She huffed. "No."

"Well, at least you haven't lost your stubborn quality. I think you should let me distract you, though. I think it'll help you sleep. You're the one who actually has to work tomorrow. We don't have to do anything."

I started counting in my head again. Begging with my own subconscious that she would let me help her in *some* way—even if it was a bit of a toxic request. And praying, even more than that, that it would somehow, in some way, lessen her anger and hatred towards me.

I was a piece of shit, I had then realized. Because I wanted her to forgive me so badly that I was willing to put the only slice of trust and fragility I was being handed.

"If we do this..." she started, and I found myself holding my breath, even as my thumb traced circles on her shirt-covered abdomen, "it's just for tonight. Nothing is going to change between us. You still hurt me, and I still hate a large piece of you. Okay?"

Like fucking hell this will only be for tonight.

My hands moved down to her lower stomach anyway. "Okay."

"And we'll still talk tomorrow. All three of us. And you may still have to sign divorce papers. Because you fucked up, and I don't know if I can ever forgive you."

My heart raced. I was never going to sign those fucking papers.

My mouth fed her the lies she needed to move past the hump anyway. "Okay."

"I...I don't know what you want to do."

I let out a heavy breath as I smoothly rolled on top of her. I braced the majority of my weight on my palms, closing in around her head. Our gaze met in the dark—a tandem of angst, pain, sadness, anger, and raw need flitting through the both of us. I swept my eyes from the top of her head, still in adorable, albeit messier, space buns, before stopping at her plush lips. "You just lay there and look pretty. This isn't about me. Okay?"

"Okay."

My mouth crashed down to hers before she could get another word in.

Chapter 7

ESTRELLA

I couldn't help the moan that escaped my throat at the feeling of Zack's mouth on mine, nor the rough texture of his beard against my face. The kiss only lasted mere moments—hardly enough time for anything—and yet, I still found myself arching towards him and wanting more.

I fucking hated kissing people.

It was more intimate than sex could ever be, in my eyes. It was choosing company, longing, and sensuality over lust and pleasure.

But with Zack...I found myself wanting more. I needed more.

So, in my handbook of dumb decisions I had made in the same twenty-four hours alone, I decided another one couldn't hurt. I pulled Zack down towards me again, our mouths moved in a hurried, frenzied fashion. I pulled at his short hair to feel him and consume him at the exact same time.

Fuck, I had missed him.

Just for tonight, I reminded myself. *Just to distract your-self from the fear of tonight.*

Yet, I was now terrified for a whole new reason. Because if I was even enjoying that kiss…I don't know how I could ever walk away again.

Zack broke our kiss with a sad chuckle. My eyebrows pinched in confusion. "I can feel you thinking too hard, *mi Estrella.* Just enjoy it. Leave your thoughts in the thunderstorm."

"I can't help it."

He sighed. "I know, baby. Let me take them away for you then."

"O-Okay. How are you going to do that?"

His smile was borderline evil. "Do you want my play-by-play, or do you want me to just take the thoughts out of your beautiful head? Because I can go into detail about everything I want to do to you, if you prefer that route."

I immediately shook my head as heat flamed across my face. "Nope. No, I'm good. You don't need to do that."

He nodded. "Thought so. Sit up."

"What?"

"Sit up," Zack demanded with an eyebrow arched as he sat back on his haunches. "I can't distract you very well if you're fully clothed, ya know. But I could always try. That would be a fun challenge, actually."

My jaw tightened. "Don't be an asshole. I'll go right back into the bedroom an—"

"And what?" he cut me off with a challenging tone. "Rub one out yourself while your husband is ready to make you cum harder than you could ever manage to do on your own?"

"Fuck you!" I exclaimed, sitting up angrily. I was ready to shove him to the floor and go back to staying drunk the entire weekend to numb my pain. "God, this was a fucking mistake. Don't talk to me like I'm one of your submissive fans that you've probably fucked on similar couches."

In seconds, my shirt was easily wrestled off of me and thrown to the floor. I gasped as the cold night air hit my skin, forcing my nipples to pebble immediately. I barely had any time to properly react. Zack was immediately above me once again, with our shocked, angry faces at war with one another. One of his hands rubbed at my bare stomach tenderly. "No bra? That's alright. It wasn't going to last long anyway, either."

I couldn't tell if the shaking coursing through my body was from rage, fear, or the cold then. "*Te odio.*"

"I love you. And you love me."

My breath caught at the fierceness in his words. Yet disbelief and fear danced around my skull anxiously. "How can I believe you?"

"Do you trust me?"

A brittle chuckle escaped my mouth. "No."

"You're lying."

"No, I'm not."

He shook his head before I felt his hand move up my body and land on my throat. My eyes widened as his hand wrapped around the column of my slender neck and squeezed the sides in a possessive hold.

He was choking me. And I...wasn't afraid.

Fuck.

Instead, my legs moved to squeeze close as arousal

hit me like a truck—only to squeeze against the sides of one of his legs instead.

The smile that took over his face was downright sinister. "Look at *mi Estrella*. Says she doesn't trust me, yet becomes needy when I take all the power from her. Isn't that right, baby?"

Somehow, even with his grip on me, I was able to squeeze out, "No."

His eyes rolled in annoyance.

I thought my answer would get him to back off, but I should have known better as he squeezed harder and leaned in closer to my face. "My love, I am going to set the record straight on something—right here, right now. I haven't fucked another woman besides you since I was thirty. I have been completely celibate and faithful to you for the entire time I've been away from you. So, if you ever—and I mean ever—compare yourself to a whoring fan again, I will bruise your ass black and blue. You are not them, and I am not one of those guys, either. Do you understand me?"

Tears immediately stung my eyes at his words, and I fear they fell down my face as he lessened the pressure of his hold against my throat marginally. He swallowed roughly and watched as they fell down my face.

I shook my head. "Yo-You haven't...?"

"No."

"Why?"

His hand finally left my throat as he wiped the tears away from my face with the pad of his thumb, ignoring my question entirely. His gaze, heavy with longing and sadness, traced every bare piece of me that he could reach. "There was never a thought of anything potentially 'after' you. There was only you. There *is* only you."

"Zack..."

"No. We'll talk tomorrow. You can ask anything tomorrow. You can hate me tomorrow. Right now?" He shook his head again before he shifted his weight down, dragging the duvet with him and popped open the waistband of my denim shorts. "Right now, I am going to tongue-fuck my wife until she's screaming, and then cuddle her to sleep. Like I have wanted to do every single day for the last decade."

700
52x
80
CD-R

Chapter 8

THEO

My dick actually *ached* in my hand as Estrella's moans, even light with her attempts to be quiet, spilled from underneath the crack of the room's door. It didn't stop my hand from continuing its languid, messy strokes, though. I groaned softly as I held it at the base, squeezing and watching a drop of precum bead at the tip.

"Fuck, Zack," Estrella whispered and moaned as I picked up my head up and strained to hear more. "Why does that feel so good? Holy shit. *Holy shit.* Fuck, it feels way too good."

I heard Zack's mocking laugh clear as day. "I know how to take care of my baby. You getting close, baby girl? You wanna cum on my fingers or tongue?"

"Tongue!" she moaned.

My cock twitched at her answer. God, I wanted to see her shake so fucking bad.

Immediately, my mind pulled to the memory of the few times I had caught her and Zack fooling around years ago. They had no shame regarding their intentions of fooling around in public, and while it grossed me out in the beginning...it only made me hornier and hornier as time went on.

I decided early only that something had to be wrong with me.

I had researched exactly why I enjoyed it so much in the beginning. Hyper-fixated on it, even. Something had to be wrong with me for me to enjoy watching my brother—my own flesh and blood—make his girlfriend cream on his own cock. Time spent on research and forums had suggested voyeurism.

Turns out that if I couldn't be a performer, I would be a watcher instead.

That it was natural for human beings to enjoy the sight of each other in intense pleasure. That it merely scratched at a primal part of our brains.

It didn't explain the jealousy, though. The intense, aching, *over-consuming* jealousy.

And then the day came when I caught her masturbating by herself. Twenty-years-old, a stark contrast to my thirty-years-old self at the time, watching her spread her summer-tanned legs and stuff her pretty, wet pussy with her own fingers through the crack of Zack's bedroom door. Her hair, as long and curly as it was in the present, spilled around her as her back arched and her breaths came out in silent little puffs.

I was a fucking pervert.

But it was the hottest thing I had witnessed in my entire life.

And when I watched through the crack of Zack's bedroom door, my hand fumbled through the zipper of my jeans and took out my cock, stroking and aching, just as I was now hearing Zack eating her out in the damned hotel.

She never saw me. Hell, she never even realized I had the personification of an adult crush on her while my brother talked about proposing for weeks—let alone that I was down bad enough to watch her masturbate through the crack of a door.

I should have been an adult and walked away. Not watched. Not touch myself.

But I didn't do either of those things. And those moans and spasms had haunted me every single day for years.

I would be damned if I didn't get to witness them again. Especially given the fact that the future was extremely undetermined, and if my last chance to see Estrella cum was at the hands of my brother once again... then so be it.

I kicked off my boxers entirely as I stood up—fist still moving in languid strokes as I crept silently toward the door—only to oh-so-quietly turn the knob and crack the door open a few inches.

The sight before me made my knees go weak, and I leaned against the door frame for support.

Estrella's legs were wrapped tightly around Zack's head as he tongue fucked our girl to hell and back. One of her hands pulled at his short hair as her hips shifted into him, mewls leaving her throat, as the other scratched down his back. Even in the dark, with their features hardly unrecognizable, I could still make out the sight of her legs shaking. I would bet our entire band's equity that she was mere moments away from crossing the finish line.

It was that realization that had me turning my languid strokes into quick, heavy ones. I heard the soft slapping sounds of my hand against my own length, meaning they probably could, too, if they stopped for even a second, but I somehow didn't find it in me to care at that moment.

If things worked out in our favor, I was here to stay. Right in their dynamic.

If things worked out against our favor, neither of us would probably see Estrella again.

Fuck it.

Zack groaned as his own hips shifted into the couch marginally. "C'mon, baby girl. Give it to me. I know you're right there."

"Fuck, fuck, fuck, fuck! Tell me something. Anything. Just—fuck—*talk.*"

Immediately, I felt a tingle go up my own spine at the sound of her begging and whining, and my balls drew heavy and tight soon after. I squeezed my hand against my length even more, craving the feeling of her spasming pussy around me desperately.

My brother's wife.

But my princess, too.

Zack's forearm shifted as he added another finger to the mix. I couldn't tell how many digits were inside of her, but regardless—between the additional stretch and the presumed curling, her moans only got louder, and my breathing only got ragged.

I wanted to come with her, though. Even as my abdomen flexed tightly.

Zack's voice was rough. "I'm never letting you go again, *mi Estrella*. Theo is never letting you go again, either. You belong to us. You are ours. And one day," his hand moved up to firmly press against her lower abdomen, forcing her to let out a scream of pleasure at the added sensation, "one day, you'll take us both until you're carrying our baby, too. So, give me this fucking orgasm now, before you don't have a choice in the matter at all."

Fuck.

That was hot.

I watched as she fell off the cliff. Her back bowed under the intensity of her orgasm, moans and gasps pouring out of her. And like a puppet being pulled under *both* of their strings, I followed immediately after. Fire licked up my spine as my cock pulsed in my hand, cum dripping from the head of my length and onto the floor. I couldn't contain the guttural moan and pant that escaped my mouth from the pleasure.

I forced my hand to keep moving on my length, milking every ounce of pleasure out of my system that I could. I was no stranger to masturbating, but I could have sworn that was the best orgasm I had in years. And, looking down, I watched as my own seed spread itself on my dick with the movements, forcing yet another groan through my mouth.

What I would have given to have my princess on her

knees, cleaning up the mess she made, while Zack watched for once instead.

As moments passed, my hand stopped its pumping, and I gripped the door frame to steel myself. The pair mere feet away from me had gone silent—nothing more than ragged breathing and pants filling the space—and I knew I had to move before one of them called me *or* my pitiful cum puddle out.

Fuck.

Except, when I finally found the courage to look up, I found Estrella's face pointed in my exact direction, rather than down at Zack.

My heart leapt directly into my throat.

Double fuck.

I knew my choice was a risk, but fuck me for thinking it wouldn't have any consequences at all. For thinking I could hide in the dark like a loser all the same. For thinking I would go by unnoticed like I had all those years ago.

Our gazes stayed locked.

It was far too dark to see her facial expression. Though—of all fucking sounds to make—a giggle tinkled the air, followed by a soft moan as she stretched. Seconds passed and I was surprised that I hadn't begun to feel a tingling in my left arm from the potential cardiac arrest of the situation.

I watched as her hand glided through Zack's hair softly, in an almost reassuring and comforting gesture, as her face stayed staring directly at the spot me and my limp dick stood.

And when neither of us made a move to speak or move, I knew I had to be the bigger person.

I couldn't scare her away.

Not after everything I had already done.

I shifted backwards a few steps before softly closing the door in both of our faces.

Chapter 9

THEO

"**N**ope!" I called out, right as I exited my bedroom and saw Estrella tip-toe towards the elevator that would lead her towards her inevitable and *rude* exit. She froze like a deer in headlights as I swiftly walked towards her, grabbed her gently by her elbow, and pulled her towards the kitchenette that had come with that particular suite's booking. "Nah, nah, nah. No sneaking out, little miss. Not until you eat something to settle all the alcohol you had yesterday."

She stubbornly huffed and crossed her arms. "I don't need to eat. I'm not even hungover."

"And I don't care."

"Like you didn't care about being a Peeping Tom last night? Or are we just going to pretend that didn't happen?"

I should have known that she would bring it up right off the bat. I merely shrugged and smirked as I looked around the fridge. This hotel was so bougie that it even went as far as to stock their *pantries*. I was positive that the prices of the ingredients were easily five-times what they would have been in an actual grocery store, but I merely shrugged as I grabbed everything needed to make pancakes.

The pros of being one of the best bands in the industry? The cost of things wasn't necessarily a concern. Even if our bookkeeper occasionally growled every now and then. The cons of it, though? I had spent years eating solely fast food from hundreds of tour buses, and I would rather croak than subject myself to that torture again.

It was worth the growling bookkeeper and probable twenty-dollar carton of milk.

"I beg to differ. Your breath stinks, your eyes are bloodshot, and your hands have a little tremor to them. You need electrolytes and glucose." I turned back to her and pointed at her cropped shirt next. "And that's cheating. Obsidian Static? I thought you were photographing Neon Cherry today. If you're gonna cheat, at least wear our merch."

"Since when did you become such a health geek?" She looked down at her shirt and pouted. "And the drummer gave this to me personally. Don't be a hater."

I shrugged and ignored the last part of her sentence. "Sometime over the last eight years, probably."

I hid my smile by turning my back when her blatant scoff met my ears.

That was probably not the best thing to say, but ultimately, I was right. She needed to eat. And I would use every single excuse I could to get her to stay with me for a few extra minutes. Or hours, for that matter. And as I began measuring the milk and flour, my shoulders sagged in relief at the sound of the dining chair being pulled out.

"You're not my dad, ya know."

I barked out a laugh loud enough to wake up a snoring Zack mere feet away from us. "Nah, I'm not. And while the thought of you calling me Daddy isn't all that bad, I know for a fact that Mr. Flores would have my head. So, I'll behave myself on that one."

Zack's hoarse and sleepy voice sounded next. "Why are you the one that gets to claim the title of Daddy? I'm the older one."

I turned around to let out my own sarcastic quip. Though, as I turned around, it was cut short when I saw Estrella's face, filled with sadness and pain, her hand gripping the countertop as though she were about to float away. Immediately, the mixture of eventual pancake mix was left forgotten on the countertop. I walked towards her before lowering myself into a squat and reaching up to grip her chin with my fingers. Tears lined her eyes. "Hey, hey, hey. What's going on? What happened?"

She sniffed and tried to pull away from me. My fingers only tightened their hold. "It's nothing. I'm fine."

I felt Zack's presence at my back before he spoke. My eyes stayed trained on Estrella, though. "It's obviously not nothing, *mi Estrella*. We were just joking."

Her eyebrows pinched together, forcing a singular tear to leak down her face. "Right. Because let's just joke and talk about my dad as if he's still alive. Stellar joke, guys. Appreciate you."

"What?" My heart could have stopped beating then and there. "What did you just say?"

She picked her head up, her eyes locking in on mine quizzically before jumping up to Zack's features. I didn't know what his expression looked like, but I would have bet money that it was similar to my own. "*Papá*. He's dead. You didn't know?"

I shook my head fiercely. "No. We had no idea."

Zack spoke immediately after, and it was only then that I turned my face back to look at him. Horror coated every single one of his features. "When? How?"

Estrella shrugged as if she hadn't just thrown a time bomb directly at both of us. "Three years ago. Heart attack. He was too stubborn to even call for help. You knew how he was. That never changed. He was gone before any of us could do anything about it."

Fucking hell.

Even with everything we had done to try to keep tabs on our girl through out the years.

It wasn't nearly enough if we still missed something like that.

"I'm so...so fucking sorry, princess."

Zack joined in. "I'm so sorry. I genuinely had no idea. I would have been there if I did."

That got a sarcastic laugh as she pulled out of my touch entirely. She swiveled the chair back in the direction of the cooktop and bowl of batter, ignoring us entirely. I flinched as her next set of words dug deep into everything I was. "Right. Because my dead *papá* would have been the action to get your head out of your ass and choose me. That makes me feel so much fucking better about myself, thanks."

"Th-That's not what I meant, *mi Estrella*."

"Whatever. Just make breakfast, Theo. Neon Cherry plays in the next few hours, and I have a date with their makeup artist before the show begins. And we still need to get this talk out of the way, don't we?"

I nodded my head as though she were looking at me.

She wasn't, though.

I didn't deserve her attention at all after that one.

We found ourselves on the couch an hour later as an awkward silence fell over all three of us. Estrella dragged her pancakes along the plate, playing in the syrup. Though, she did manage to take a bite here and there, which I was extremely grateful for. She was thin and I was desperate for real food to touch her stomach.

Finally, she broke the silence as she looked up at Zack. "Are you going to sign the divorce papers?"

His answer was immediate. "No."

"Why not? I don't want your money. I will tell a divorce court the same in a nano-second."

"I know you don't. And even if you did, and we had no other choice, I would give it to you."

She placed the plate of her half-eaten pancakes on the coffee table. I reined in the sigh that I wanted to make. "I am already as humble as I could possibly be right now. I have felt nothing but aching loneliness, sadness, and confusion for years. No matter the alcohol and sex, it has never gone away. So, for fuck's sake, just tell me why you have the balls to run away from me—from us—yet not enough to actually leave me in all areas of the definition. I deserve that much."

Zack's voice grew heavy with emotion, and I looked up to see his eyes holding nothing but longing as he stared back at her. "Because I never wanted to leave you in the first place. I never wanted to run. But...I had to."

"Why? Fucking *why*?"

My voice cut through their growing tension. "Because of me."

The silence that followed was thick.

Zack and I had fought for years. We had almost destroyed not only ourselves, but our career, too. All because I was a selfish bastard who wanted what I couldn't have, and held a stupid as fuck ultimatum over him.

Estrella, or the record deal of a lifetime.

Estrella, the girl I thought we could both get over...or the possibility of fame, fortune, happiness, and so much more. And when you were each other's only family at that point, with your own parents having died in your twenties, it was the most manipulative ask ever.

And it worked.

I was such a fucking idiot.

My voice was hoarse as I continued. "He left you because of me. Because I have been irrevocably in love with you for years. Almost as much as he is. And I was a spoiled fucking brat who couldn't bear to witness someone getting something I wanted so, so badly. So, I essentially forced him to leave you. I threw our record deal in his face. I threw his only passion and career in his own face. And then I forced us both to turn our backs on you. Thinking...thinking it would do something, I guess. And that all three of us could just move the fuck on."

Estrella stared at me, saying nothing.

Zack cut in next. "I never wanted to leave you. But the record deal was already signed. I had planned to tell you, and then...shit hit the fan. My hands felt tied. I-I didn't know what to do. But I need you to know that I regret choosing this life over you every single day since then."

Estrella's eyes stayed on me.

The blankness in them tore me apart about as much as her silence did.

I kept talking. "On your wedding day, I lied to you. I never told him that I had kissed you at that stupid party. That I had professed my love to you then, too, but we were too far gone to remember. I never told him anything until months later. I...I only told you. Begging and wondering if I could get you to choose me over him. Like an absolute dumbass."

Silence.

Complete and utter silence.

I probably should have skipped breakfast, too, like her. I was afraid it was going to come back up between the anxiety and fear coursing through me.

"*Mi Estrella*, plea—"

"*Don't!*"

I blinked at the shout.

She shook her head angrily. "I have spent years

wondering why I wasn't good enough by someone who called me his soulmate on a nearly nightly basis. I have begged God and back for an answer—to the point that I stopped believing in him entirely. I have drowned myself in alcohol and sex as a distraction for *years* to try and prove to myself that I was worth more than abandonment. Only for what?" She laughed incredulously. "Only for my husband and brother-in-law to tell me that they both have been madly in love with me the whole time, only to torture me for shits and giggles?"

"Please," I started. "Please don't call me your brother-in-law. I don't want that."

"Then what *the fuck* do you want? What do either of you want from me? Because it sure as fuck doesn't sound like I'm getting out of my marriage anytime soon."

Zack answered on a rough swallow. "We both want you. We want you to be...ours."

We both watched as Estrella's mouth opened and closed like a fish at the admission.

I spoke before she could have the chance to do so herself, even as my gaze averted itself to her half-eaten plate. "I could never get over you. And Zack hasn't even looked at another woman in years, let alone thought about the possibility of someone else. And after a really bad fist fight that landed us both in the hospital, and nearly in jail, we just realized...Princess, there is only ever you. You *own* us. And you somehow have the power to both make and destroy us. Even if you don't want us at all."

It could have been hours before she spoke. But when she did, I knew instantly that she was crying. "So, what?

I'm the birthday present little kids fought over before they realized that sharing is caring? Really?"

"Estrella, no. That's not what we're saying," Zack protested.

"Sure sounds like it. Theo?"

I didn't have the heart to lie to her anymore. "Yeah. Yeah, pretty much. But on my terms. I ruined it all. He didn't do anything wrong, except choose me when he should have left me in the dust."

"Nice. I'm not a human being with emotions, but instead a fucking toy for brothers to fight over. How fucking wonderful. Do I even get a say in any of this whatsoever?"

"Of course you do."

The sound of her footsteps leading to the elevator forced me to look up. I hadn't even known she was standing, let alone making a run for it. Zack called out to her, but she only shook her head as her finger jammed into the elevator button.

"Estrella," I croaked. "Please, just...give us a chance. Give us a chance to make it up to you."

She turned back towards us abruptly. "You know what the funny thing is? If I had known this all those years ago, I maybe would have even considered it. Because I loved Theo deeply. Like a true brother then, but I could have made that love transfer into something more. I could have *tried*. But now? Is it even worth it? How can I trust either of you ever again? To make me fall in love—to heal me—only to leave me in the dust again."

"We're s—"

She looked at Zack directly. "I wanted children. I

wanted a life with you. And you both took that from me. Without even thinking about me at all. Sorry isn't going to fucking cut it."

"We'll show you. We'll work for it. We're never going anywhere again. I swear. Just...let us prove it to you. Some way. Somehow."

Her head shook, forcing her curls to sweep over her shoulder. "I need to go to work."

Zack begged next. "Please, baby. We'll do anything."

She paused as she turned to the elevator, waiting for it to open for her. I waited with a baited breath.

"Anything?" Her voice croaked.

"Anything."

"Fucking *grovel* like your life depends on it then. Chase me. Make me feel actually *wanted*. Because even though Theo fucked everything up—*you're* the one who still chose him, Zack. *You're* the one who was too much of a fucking coward to kick him to the curb and choose your so-called *soulmate*." Her voice was thick with emotion as she took a deep breath. "If anything, I *should* choose him. Just to show you how it feels to be kicked to the curb and chosen second."

My head hung in shame as the elevator doors opened, only for them to close and take her away from us.

Zack nudged my shoulder with his before he stood, refusing to let me bury myself in my thoughts. "You heard our girl. Get up. Get ready. We're gonna chase her until she's sick of us. *Both* of us."

"You seem...so cool," Hale started, stuttering on a breath as she began blending the dark eyeshadow into my crease. "Like, you're a badass photographer *and* you're married to the lead singer of From Stars to Evolution?! Do you know how lucky and cool that makes you? Can I literally *be* you?"

I laughed as I peeked open the eye she wasn't working on to take her in, only to laugh harder once I saw the bright red blush on her face. Paired with her shoulder-length, brown hair, it suited her—and the cinnamon roll personality only highlighted it. "I mean, after the fight I just had with them, I may let you have 'em. They're annoying and stupid."

"No way! God, I already have to keep up with my own boys. Not to mention, while I love me some divorced-dad-rock, those men are definitely too old for me." The hand doing my eyeshadow paused, and I giggled again at the outright call-out of their ages. "No offense! Age gap is cool and all. I'm just...not that into it. And like, ya know, they're hot and all bu—"

I placed my hand on her arm in a reassuring squeeze. "Hey, hey. It's cool. They're ancient as fuck. I'm surprised they can still squat without breaking their knees. No worries."

Hale nodded. Yet, confusion hit me as I watched her blushed even harder out of nowhere. Dread settled in my stomach immediately when she peeked around me, and the sound of Zack's voice only worsened it. "Oh, really now? You hear that, Theo? We are *ancient*."

Theo's voice joined him. "Damn. That hurt, princess. You wound me."

My shoulders slumped.

I was emotionally wrecked and tired.

Blowing up on men was generally a fun past-time of mine, but when I had to blow up on the men I apparently loved enough to even think about giving a second chance?

Woof.

I kept my eyes on Hale, refusing to give them the time of day. While eyeshadow was generally first in her order of operations, I was unbelievably grateful that I had begged her to go with a more basic look. We only had mascara and lipstick left, and then I could get the fuck away from them and continue my brooding in peace before the show.

Hale shuddered under their presence all the same. I almost pitied her. She was damn good at her job—she wouldn't be here if that weren't the case, regardless of her connections—but she was young, and that rockstar power would throw anyone innocent and kind for a loop. "It's...uh, nice to meet you...?"

I flinched as Zack's hand came to my right, followed by Theo on my left.

How the fuck did I not notice they were that close to me?

"Zack Anderson," Zack said, right as Theo introduced himself as well.

My eyes rolled.

Polite motherfuckers.

Hale blushed furiously as she somehow reached for both of their hands. "Uhm. Yeah. Hi! I'm Hale. Lead makeup designer for Neon Cherry. It's nice to meet y'all!"

Zack laughed lightly. "It's nice to meet you, too. How'd our girl talk you into doing her makeup?"

"Not your girl!" I interrupted.

Everyone ignored me as Hale responded. "Oh, she didn't even ask! I met her a few days ago when she did a different set of photography for us. Her and Derek hit it off really well, and ya know, he's the complete broody asshole of the group—so, I figured if she could crack him, we could definitely be friends too. She's...really, really cool."

Zack's hand landed on my shoulder with a gentle squeeze. "Yeah. She is really cool. I like her a lot. Major crush and all."

Fuck my stupid genetics and hormones for forcing me to blush furiously. Hale and I were about to be twinzies.

"What're you guys doing here?" I ground out. I needed to try to gain control of my beating heart somehow, and being closed off was generally the way to do that. "I told you both I was working."

Theo leant down to whisper in my ear, yet absolutely failed at making his whisper an actual private moment. "You really thought we'd let you leave the conversation how you did with no follow-up? We're here to see you in action, princess. I wanna see you work." Hale choked on a breath as she heard him speak, but smothered it with a cough as she continued digging in her makeup bag.

Zack leant down to whisper as well. "I don't know when you'll grasp this, but chasing you is my favorite activity, pretty girl. I've been doing it for a couple years now. Just doing what you asked for."

Heat licked up my spine, and I genuinely couldn't tell if it was anger or pleasure. "How supportive of you, darling," came my sarcastic reply.

Moments passed as Hale finished up my makeup look, pairing the simplistic eyeshadow with multiple coats of mascara and an old mauve shade of lipstick that complimented my complexion beautifully. When she handed the mirror, I pouted at my own reflection and complimented her work.

She made me look stunning.

"Alright!" Hale said, snatching the mirror away from me with a giggle. "Show starts in twenty minutes. Go get us some sexy photos. But...please, not too sexy. I'm already thinking that this weekend is going to be one of the horniest of my life, and the testosterone around me is blinding enough as is."

I laughed deeply, along with Zack and Theo, before nodding and going to collect my camera bag and wristbands for security access. To get the best shots in the industry, I practically had to hump the security men, and therefore needed even more clearance than just the general VIP wristbands.

I didn't make it more than ten steps before Zack's hand landed on my shoulder again. I turned to face him with an eyebrow raise. His voice was gravely as he spoke. "Uhm. Derek?"

I shook my head. "Don't worry about anything more than what it was."

He nodded with a smile. But then I couldn't contain the jab, paired with another combative eyebrow raise. Humbling this man was refreshing after so many years. Even if it made me a little immature. "But, yeah. I didn't know my husband actually liked me until twelve or so hours ago, or that either of you liked me until four hours ago. Can't blame a girl for having needs, can you?"

He blinked before blushing furiously. It was almost... cute. Adorable, even. "Right. Yeah. No, you're right. The past from this moment on is the past."

And as I shrugged his hand off me to get my stuff, I could have sworn that I heard Theo say the words, "Yeah...I should've warned you about that."

My eyes rolled again as I fought a growing smile.

Men.

i'm sorry
But i will always love you. And i'll
come back for you when i'm ready.
                              Zack

Chapter 11

ZACK

She was ethereal to watch. I absolutely couldn't take my eyes off her. And as Theo stood to my right in the VIP tent to the left of the main stage, I knew he felt the exact same.

Watching her in action was probably the hottest and coolest thing I would ever bear witness to in my entire existence, regardless of anything I had seen in my time on this planet yet. Even when Derek pointed his drumsticks at her—while a strike of jealousy should have smacked me in the face—I only smiled as I watched her laugh behind the camera.

I smiled even more when she stuck her middle finger out at him, though.

"She's...something else," Theo shouted over the music. Even with our fancy ear plugs blocking out some of the music, it was still a challenge to even hear yourself think, let alone someone else.

Just as I was about to shout a response to him though, my eyes widened as I watched Estrella shout to a security guard, only for him to shrug and offer his leg. Within seconds, she was climbing the man like a damned tree right in front of everyone before she straddled his shoulders. My stomach dropped for a split second as I watched her wobble and catch her balance— at least, until the man gripped her legs to stabilize her. Unlike me, though, she laughed wildly before grabbing her camera and continuing her efforts at capturing the performance at hand.

A nervous laugh mixed in with my words as I shouted back to Theo. "Yup. That's our girl."

Almost as if she could hear me herself—impossible, even if I liked to imagine otherwise—her French braided head swiveled until her gaze honed in on mine with a bright smile.

Hope bloomed in my chest as she raised the camera again and took the shot at us, rather than her assignment at hand.

I didn't even know if I was smiling. But one thing I knew for sure?

I was as starstruck for her as our fans were for us.

And when she turned back to the stage with a shy blush, I couldn't help the hope that festered in my soul.

Theo tapped my shoulder in a brotherly manner as he kept his gaze on her, too.

No words needed spoken.

While we should have paid attention to Neon Cherry, and especially given the fact that Estrella seemed to have a personal connection to the band that could lead to beneficial partnerships in the future, I merely shrugged the thought away.

I wasn't looking away from my star ever again.

Anxiety thrummed through my entire existence as I waited for Estrella to come back from the security pit.

Only...she never came.

I looked down at my watch before peaking over at Theo. The show had ended nearly twenty minutes ago, and we had both watched her duck out as soon as the lights went down.

Where the hell was she?

"Does she always take so long? What's going on?"

Theo rolled his eyes before meeting me with a deadpan stare. "You act like either of us know her schedule or order-of-operations. Why are you asking me?"

I glared at him. Oh, how I just loved my brother sometimes.

Another guy's voice interrupted our sour stare-off. "Gentlemen. I'd say thanks for watching the show, but I have the suspicion that our music is definitely not why you're backstage and waiting. Especially when you shouldn't be here at all."

I winced as I turned towards the voice's accusation, but it was Theo's voice that drew me up short. "Hey, Derek. Regardless of the reason, you all sounded fantastic. You know, we should schedule a meeting with your agent. See if a collaboration is ever in the future?"

Derek's face lit up with a sarcastic smile. "Are you

kissing my ass because I almost beat yours last night? Or so I don't kick you out right now?"

"I absolutely am. And both."

"Noted. I just wanted to let you all know that your girl texted me. I tried to get dinner with her, but she said that she's going to go get dinner and then go back to her hotel room. That's all I know, though."

I blinked in offense before looking down at my phone. "Why didn't she text us?"

Theo growled. "Probably because she doesn't have our numbers, dumbass."

Right.

Ouch.

Derek laughed. "Bro to bro, she only sent the text five minutes ago. You can probably still find her lingering around somewhere." I was moving towards the exit instantly. Except, Derek gripped my bicep tightly as I tried to pass him. Somehow, he stood even taller over my 6'2 frame, and his beefy stature forced me to shrink back mildly. "Hey. Don't hurt her again, alright? I may not know you. I may not even know her that well. But I am a broken man myself, and broken people recognize those who are hurting even more than others. She doesn't deserve it."

I swallowed roughly and nodded my head as he let go, only for him to turn to Theo next. "That girl is a fucking saint that neither of you deserve, regardless of whatever odd polyamorous shit you have going on. And believe me when I tell you—if she dropped you both on your asses tomorrow, I'd be another man in que, begging for even a lick of attention. Fix your shit before someone treats her better."

Theo's voice was soft. "We're not gonna hurt her again."

Derek nodded before wiping at his forehead and trekking towards his band mates. "Better not. I'll kick your asses myself and let my daughter score it. I'll let our agent know they'll be hearing from you, though."

Fucking finally.

Black and green split hair.

Standing in line at some random corn dog stand, right next to a Ferris wheel that illuminated itself brightly in the darkening sky.

Of all things to eat after an entire day of working on an empty stomach, she would be the girl to choose a damn corndog. I shook my head as Theo and I both jogged towards her, ignoring the murmurs around us entirely. We were probably fucking stupid for walking around the festival without any security guards, but at the same time, it certainly wasn't the dumbest thing we had ever done, either.

Once next to her, I slung a heavy arm across her shoulders casually. She flinched at the contact and I was almost surprised she didn't swing at me as I spoke. "Man, are you a hard one to find with your height. If it weren't for this pretty hair, I never would have found you. Especially because I was looking for braids."

Theo laughed as he showed up on her other side, forcing her to flinch yet again. I bit back a smile that time. "Seriously. I like it, though. Your natural curls have always suited you."

She threw her head back against my arm exasperated. "Great. My men are stalkers. That's just wonderful. How did you even know I left?"

We both ignored that question. We weren't throwing Derek under the bus so soon. "Awe. We're your men? That sounds so much more official when it's coming from your lips instead of ours."

Her eyes rolled. "I'll take it back. Can you both go find something to do? I'm tired, horny, and hungry. I just want my hotel room now. And the nap of a lifetime."

My eyebrows quirked up immediately. "I mean, I can help with that, ya know."

"Hey, now," Theo said slyly. "Team effort, bro."

Estrella scoffed and immediately shrugged her arm off me. "Ya know what? No. No, I'm not done being angry with either of you, actually. I was trying to be nice and offer an olive branch with being at least nice and flirty, but you just *had* to go gross caveman-y on me when I'm still processing what *this* even is."

"Oh, c'mon! That was a test?" Theo exclaimed in a pout.

She whipped her head towards him in anger. I watched, expecting her to tell him off. Instead, I found myself shocked when she grabbed the neckline of his t-shirt, pulled him down roughly, and forced her mouth on his. His eyes went wide, looking at me for confirmation. When I merely tugged at my beard and shrugged, his eyes closed, and I watched as one of his hands went to cup her ass. Though, he hardly got to enjoy it for long before she was pulling away and tapping at his cheek with her hand. "Feel better?"

He swallowed, but kept his hand on her ass. "Not one bit."

"Hah! Too fucking bad." She turned her head back towards me then, while Theo stared at her dumbstruck. "Maybe I will keep this brother after all. You know my mom told me to do that on our wedding day? I should have listened."

I shook my head as I stared at her, still tugging on my beard for some sort of grounding.

I should have been marginally upset that she had just condoned us to a PR stunt of the century. But I was far too concerned about keeping a boner down instead.

That was way too hot.

She watched me quizzically. "You're not jealous?"

My face scrunched up in confusion then. "Uhm. No. Not over him, at least. Why would I be?"

She took a step back as if someone had shoved her. "Woooow. You actually meant it."

I was utterly confused now. Theo's expression matched my own, even as she still held onto his shirt. "Meant what? What are you talking about right now?"

She was whiplash incarnate.

A rolling mix of emotions ran across her face, consisting all the way from confusion, sadness, anger, and more. Her next words cut deep as she shoved Theo away, held onto the camera bag strap that was on her shoulder, and turned away, shaking her head. "Fuck you both for putting me through this like it's fucking normal. I'm going back to my hotel room, and you're not invited."

I blinked.

Theo blinked.

The man running the food stand called for us to move up so he could take our order as we watched her walk away.

And then, her words from that morning echoed in my head.

Chase me.

For the first time since I had gotten that email from Sophie, anger filled my head. Blinding hot anger and rage.

I was fucking sick of her push and pull games already.

That girl was ours ready whether she was willing to comprehend it or not.

So, no. Absolutely *not.* I was not letting her walk away from me like that. I wasn't letting her play games like that, even if we both deserved the torture. And I didn't give a fuck if I was about to be hit with the restraining order of a lifetime by my own wife. I had been a coward for years—nearly an entire decade—and I was tired of it, once and for all.

If she wanted to play a push and pull game—then she could. But it would be *with* us, rather than against us.

I jogged after her. With my long legs, I caught up to her in no time. With Theo on my heels, I grabbed her by my waist and tossed her directly over my shoulder. She squealed before I felt her hand pound at my lower back. "Let me down, you idiot!"

I landed one firm, rough smack on her ass that had her gasping. Turning to Theo, I ignored her as I asked, "Where to?"

Phones pointed at us everywhere. Our actions and words would undoubtedly be on a magazine cover by daylight. Though, somehow, I didn't give a fuck about the damage control we would have to face whatsoever.

My wife's attitude needed to be corrected.

Theo looked around, gauging the scene with us, before he nodded towards the Ferris wheel. The line was quickly diminishing, and it was certainly a better place to have the *chat* I needed to have with Estrella—compared to anywhere else at a festival like a damned porta-potty—so it was better than nothing. And regardless of this little PR spectacle, I doubted our agent would be remotely thrilled with either of us if we shoved Estrella in an Uber for the hotel.

I could see the headline then.

From Stars to Evolution kidnaps girl?!

Fuck no.

I shrugged before trudging my way back towards it. The man running the corn dog stand watched us pass by in shock, yet returned back to making someone's order when I waved and gave him a proper thumbs-up.

Theo giggled at my back before whispering. "My cabbages!"

I turned to him with a raised brow as I got behind a

couple wanting to join the Ferris wheel in front of us. "Are you seriously quoting *Avatar: The Last Airbender* right now? Of all times?"

"What? I'm just a boy. Leave me alone."

Estrella growled and hit my lower back again. I groaned that time. I was fit for my age, and carrying her was no burden to me at all, but my poor bones would snap if she kept that up. In an attempt to make her stop, I slapped her ass one more time and made sure it was hard enough to leave a sting. She whimpered against me, "God, you're such a dick."

I smirked as I met the attendee's eyes when it was our time to get on the ride. She was a young girl, probably around the age of twenty or so, and they widened dramatically as they took in our situation. Theo dug in his back pocket for his wallet before he handed her a full-fledged one-hundred dollar bill. "Pretend that this thing gets stuck when we get to the top, yeah? I'll give you another one if you make it last a solid twenty-minutes or so?"

She stuttered before taking it. "Uh-uhm. Su-sure. Okay!"

I nodded in thanks before gesturing for Theo to get in the carriage, where I immediately followed. I maneuvered the still-wiggling and growling Estrella before gently placing her in between us, right as Theo lowered the safety bar. It clicked in place, locking, and we both turned to her with a smirk.

Her face was red as a tomato as she seethed. "What the fuck?"

I tapped her jean-clad thigh before winking at the

Ferris wheel attendee. "We're gonna have a nice, good talk, *mi Estrella.*"

She shoved at my shoulder roughly. "Fuck you! I don't want to. Did that ever cross your mind? That I may actually need time to process being shared?! That it's not just a hoax?"

As the carriage began to go backwards in its motion to add any other riders, I turned to her and tugged at her hair roughly. Her head slanted at the motion, another gasp tearing out of her mouth, but I didn't miss the desire that clouded her eyes from the rough motion.

She *liked* it.

It was my turn to growl as Theo twirled his own hand into her hair. "I don't give a fuck anymore. You're going to see how good it can be. How good we can both be. Together."

Chapter 12

ESTRELLA

"You remember how much we used to fool around in public?" Zack continued as his hand tugged at my hair again, forcing a moan out of my throat. His nose skated down the length of my throat, and I knew without a doubt in my mind that he was watching Theo as he took control of me. "Figured we may as well go down memory lane while we talk. What do you think about that?"

I swallowed roughly. "I think you're both actually insane."

Theo tugged at a lock my curly hair next, gently. "Probably. But you don't hate it, do you?"

"I...I don't know."

Zack groaned. "Mmm. Okay. Your safe word is 'drumsticks' then. You gonna say it? Because we'll both stop if you do, and I'll shout to the attendee to keep it moving. You just say the word."

"D-Drumsticks?"

The laugh Theo let out was cruel. "Yeah, princess.

Your days of fucking drummers are over. You won't be needing that word any other damn thing than your safe word."

I couldn't help the sarcastic reply that came out of my mouth. "Oh, yeah? So, lead guitarists and screamers it is, then? Am I going to be fucked with a cordless mic one day? Grind my pussy into a guitar? Or is it only drumsticks that are off the table?"

Theo tugged my hair roughly next, taking me away from Zack entirely. I gasped at the rough action that had my neck craning towards him. "Don't tempt me with a good time. I would bet our entire band on the fact that we could make you feel things that none of your other little boy toys over the years have made you feel."

I blushed furiously as I looked him in the eyes. I didn't know if that was a promise or an accusation, and I felt like I needed to defend myself. "I'm not a slut."

His right eyebrow raised. "I never said you were one."

Zack tugged my hair back again, forcing my eyes on his. I was already beginning to feel so overstimulated. "But you'll be our slut. Won't you, *mi Estrella?*"

"I—"

"Say your safe word then," Theo snapped as he gripped my thigh tightly. "Say it, and I won't make you come for us right here. I won't spread your pretty little legs and make you cum on my fingers while you kiss your husband. Go on. We're waiting."

I opened my mouth to say it. To prove them wrong.

To prove to myself that I was stronger than the men that had held onto me for years.

Heat bloomed to my cheeks furiously when no sound

came out of my throat. Instead, my eyes just danced between the both of them in embarrassment. And in an embarrassing amount of need.

Zack's crystal blue eyes locked on mine. "Do you want me? Yes or no. It is a very easy question to answer."

I shook my head. "You're not playing fair."

My mouth opened in shock as Theo's hand slid across my throat and held on tightly. Just like Zack's hand had done last night. Except, instead of forcing me to look at him, he forced me to look at Zack instead. "Yes or no, Estrella. We may not be playing fair—but you certainly didn't play fair yourself when you kissed me to try to make him jealous, even when we told you that we both wanted you. We tried being nice, but you had to be a little brat. So, be a good girl now and answer the *fucking* question."

Zack's mouth watched mine eagerly, and my tongue darted out to lick my lips.

I was still pissed.

I'd probably be pissed, bratty, and hurt for a very long time.

But fuck. I already knew the answer. I had known the answer the second that I was reassigned to that damn festival.

"Yes. I've always wanted you. I'm just...really fucking scared."

"I know," he whispered back. "And I know I have so much to make up for. But let me start here."

Theo released my throat before squeezing in closer to me and placing a kiss at the top of my head. I shivered beneath both of their gazes. Except, when I tried to duck away from them, it was Zack's hand that moved to my throat next, and he angled my head right at Theo. "Do you want him, too? Do you want Theo?"

My thoughts scrambled on a dime as Zack's hold tightened.

That question was far, far harder for me to process.

Did I want Theo? Did I want my husband's brother, who should have been my brother, too, by law? Did I want to risk everything with my needs?

My mind flashed back to just last night, once again.

To the sight of Theo standing there, with his cock in his hand and dripping cum on the floor, and how I hadn't been turned off in the slightest. Even while Zack continued licking at me. In fact, I had wondered if it had turned me on even more—when I had heard the sound of him moaning but had refused to look up to confirm my thoughts. Let alone when the groan from his orgasm had hit my ears, mixing with my own orgasm in the most sinful way.

Zack had moaned into my pussy then, too. He *knew*. But he just kept going.

They really did want this.

Tears filled my eyes at the realization. My voice was hoarse when I spoke. "Yeah. Yeah, I think I do."

Theo's hands didn't hesitate before they were at the button of my jeans, snapping them open. His eyes stayed on mine as he responded. "Kiss me like you fucking mean it then. Not just to make him jealous. Show me."

And that time, when I tugged at his shirt to bring him

as close as possible—Zack's hand still on my throat in a possessive hold—I meant it with everything that I was. Our mouths clashed furiously, and it was mere seconds before our tongues battled each other's next. Moans tore from the both of us at the pent-up need, and Zack's groan as he kissed my shoulder and watched only added to it.

Fuck, how I ached to sit in his lap. To genuinely show him how much I did want him.

Even if I shouldn't want him at all.

While Zack watched, content, knowing I was still his, too.

Theo broke our kiss first. We both heaved for oxygen as we stared at each other. Yet, I couldn't stop staring at his lips for more. It was both erotic and obsessive all at once. And I found that no part of me regretted it whatsoever.

Theo grunted. "Good girl. Now, kiss your husband."

Zack's hand on my throat disappeared as I turned towards him. I didn't have a second to even grip him, to bring him closer, before his mouth was on mine—swallowing my moans. My hand moved to cup the back of his head feverishly. To bring him as close as possible. Though, I halted entirely when I felt Theo pulling at my jeans.

"Wha-What're you doing?" I asked, choking on my own throat.

Zack chuckled as his lips moved down to my neck.

Theo's hand pulled at my jeans again as he smirked. "Help me get these off. Just to your ass so the world doesn't get the show of a lifetime. I'm gonna make you cum on my fingers, right here, right now. You can choose which one of us you want to fuck more after that, princess. When you come back to *our* hotel room for the night."

Chapter 13

THEO

Estrella stuttered on her next set of words as Zack and I both tried to wrangle her jeans down slightly for better access. "I—what? I'm going back to your room with both of you?"

Zack almost looked offended. "Obviously. I'm your husband. Where did you think you were sleeping?"

I groaned deep in my throat when she lifted her ass to help us out. The sight of her black, lace panties entered my line of sight, and I was grateful that I was sitting, or else my knees absolutely would have buckled. I wanted so badly to see her nude, but I didn't need some stalker fan to see her bare pussy yet—even if we were pretty much in the damn sky—so I had to settle with that sight first.

My hand came to press over the entire front of her, and I grunted when I found her hot and wet already. She continued on a low moan. "By myself? Like, normal, I guess?"

I snorted as I pressed into her more firmly, craving her heat. "Nope. Not allowed. Never allowed again."

"Excuse me? I have a rule book now?"

I took my eyes off of her pussy long enough to make eye contact with her. Wasn't what we were doing supposed to be an attitude correction? "There is no rule book for us other than the following statements: you are ours, and ours alone, and you will never be alone again. Not like that. Are we clear, princess?"

She blushed once again.

I loved seeing her blush for me. It was euphoric.

"O-Okay."

I smiled as I looked back down at her pussy. Fuck, I needed to taste her somehow before I was nice and let her come. "Rub your clit for me, pretty girl. Show me how you like it being done."

She listened immediately. Shyly, she lowered one of her hands until they breached the hem of the lace, and I watched in rapt attention as she used her middle and ring finger in tandem—rubbing in tight, fast little circles. Immediately, her breath started to grow heavy, and I found myself achingly hard. And as Zack lowered his hand to grip himself, I knew that he was in the exact same boat that I was in.

"That's a good girl. Now, give me those fingers."

She pouted. "Why?"

I nearly growled the words at her. "Because I had to watch Zack tongue fuck you last night, and now I want a taste. Give me your damn fingers."

Zack's laugh hit my ears as she took her hand out of her panties. I moaned deeply then, seeing how they were utterly glistening. She hadn't even actually fingered herself, either, which meant she was fucking soaked. Before she had the chance to give them to me herself though—Zack delicately grabbed her wrist and fed them to me.

I hardly blinked before I was sucking them into my mouth and groaning in relief. I was sure my eyes nearly rolled to the back of my head, too.

Zack teased me as his grip left her wrist. Yet, my own hand replaced it as I slid my tongue in between her fingers, eager to take everything I could get. "I knew I heard you. Did you enjoy the show at least, you pervert?"

I released her fingers with a pop. "Made a huge mess on the floor and everything. All while thinking about our girl cock worshiping me clean."

He let out an exhaled breath. "Oof. Well, that's hot."

Estrella nodded firmly. "Yeah. Yup. I'm going to hell."

I snorted before lowering my hand beneath her panties myself this time. Just like her, I angled my hand so that my middle and ring finger pressed directly against her clit, and I relished in the low moan she let out immediately. "Yeah, princess? I think we may be going to hell with you then."

Zack grunted all of a sudden, and I looked away from what I was doing, just to see Estrella palming his dick print through his jeans. "Fuck, *mi Estrella*, Maybe don't do that?"

I smiled when Estrella merely raised a brow. Yet, pleasure lightened across her face, and her mouth popped open marginally as I applied even more pressure to her clit. "Why should I? Are you going to tell me to stop?"

He immediately shook his head. "Never, baby. It's just...been a minute. That's all."

I watched them both with rapt attention as I kept moving my fingers. My voice was guttural when I spoke again. "Kiss him, Estrella. Don't just sit there looking pretty."

Zack's face pinched in pain as she did exactly what she was told, all while continuing to rub him through his jeans. He didn't fight her or remove her hand from his crotch, and it was then I already knew he was a goner.

May as well add fuel to the fire.

I leant down to whisper in her ear. Given how close we all were, I was sure that Zack could hear me, as well, but he didn't break their kiss. "Don't just rub it. Grip it while you rub it. He's big enough, yeah? Jerk your husband off through his jeans while I rub your perfect pussy."

She moaned loudly.

I couldn't have been more grateful we were surrounded by shouting people and metal music than I was in that moment.

I kept talking to both of them. My pressure on her only grow, and I watched as her back arched and her grip on Zack's length turned almost painful. They were both drunk off their own hornyness. "God, Zack. She's fucking dripping, man. I bet she's just aching to have one of our cocks stretching her out. Aren't you, pretty girl?"

She broke her kiss long enough to answer. "I thought you said I belonged to both of you. Why not both?"

I rewarded that answer of hers by sticking a digit inside of her. I hissed as her pussy sucked me in like a vise grip. The angle of what we were doing helped absolutely nothing, but in general male stupidity, my cock twitched underneath the weight of my own zipper. And as I curled it lightly, she shuddered around me entirely. "Yeah? You want us both stretching you out?"

"God, yes!"

"Oh, my. You hear that whine, Zack? I think our girl is close."

Her eyes squeezed shut as my finger continued curling itself, all while the palm of my hand pressed into her clit once again. "Yes! Yes, yes, yes. Please!"

Zack grunted. "Make her come, Theo."

I smiled as I lowered my head to kiss and suck on the side of her neck. My hand never stopped. "Don't worry, princess. We'll both fuck you. And believe me when I say...I don't care that he's my brother when it comes to you. You'll be taking both of our cocks at once by the end of the weekend."

"Fuuuuuck, Theo!"

"That's it. Come for me, baby. Come for us." I picked my head up off her neck to look at Zack next. My words to him were utterly cruel. "You gonna make it, bro?"

He shook his head, and I almost wanted to laugh as his own hips raised. "Jesus, fuck! She's making me fucking come. Holy shit."

"Oh my God!" Estrella ground out. "Yeah? Yeah, come for me. Fuck, I've missed it so much. Come with me!"

I was surprised I didn't blow in my jeans myself. From either of them.

I watched them both, eyes bouncing back and forth, as they crossed the finish line. Estrella bit on her bottom lip to silence the majority of her ecstasy, but it didn't stop her hips from rolling into my hand to soak up every spark of pleasure she could. Her hand never stopped rubbing against Zack's length, either, and I watched as his cock throbbed before his body went taunt as a bowstring, groaning softly as he blew in his own jeans.

Seconds passed as well sat in the daze of what just happened. Breaths labored and bodies stiff.

I turned to nuzzle into Estrella's neck. "You okay?"

She turned to me with a dazed, dopey smile before turning back to Zack. "Mhhhm. Are y'all okay, though?"

Zack's face was bright red. I smirked as I slowly and gently pulled away from Estrella—even if her low whine nearly had me reconsidering. "I literally...just came...in my own pants. Like a teenager."

I snorted. "That's what you get for being celibate for eight years."

Estrella turned to me with an eyebrow raise. "And how long has it been since you've had sex?"

It was my turn to blush as Zack snorted. "Uhm, two years. Since we sent you that first ticket."

She hummed against a smirk before shifting slightly to raise her jeans back into place. "I bet you twenty bucks that you don't last more than fifteen minutes when it's your turn to fuck me then."

"I don't need twenty bucks."

She huffed with another one of her classic eyerolls. "Fine, you pretentious asshole. I bet you on your statement from earlier, then. Last more than fifteen minutes, and I'll let you both fuck me at the same time this weekend."

My gaze slid to Zack.

He shrugged.

The fucker.

"You're on, princess."

Zack groaned then before rubbing his temples with one of his hands. "I need a new pair of pants."

"Hey, at least they're black. You can't even tell."

He lowered his hands to glower at me. "I can tell."

Estrella squealed as the Ferris wheel started moving all of a sudden.

Thank fuck it hadn't started when I was knuckle deep in our girl. That would have been a story for the entire fairground. And then some.

"Hey, guys?" Estrella started, staring off into the distance. "Is...is someone having sex on that balcony?"

I turned my head in the direction of where she was staring. "Yup."

Zack's resounding groan came next. "I'm too old for all of this."

I slung my arm across the back of the carriage as I sat back to enjoy the rest of the ride. And when we passed the attendee, I winked again, and swore to float her another bill—even if doing so would be considered far too extra. "Well, party up, Gramps. We still need to grab dinner, and I have a bet with your wife to hone in on."

We hardly made it five steps into the elevator before I was pushed against one of the walls by Zack's tall figure. I craned my neck up at him as he stared down at me, and I couldn't help but run my smart aleck mouth once again. "How are those jeans? Soggy? Are you chafing? Poor baby must be so uncomfortable."

He shook his head at me before I felt his hands slide under my ass. In seconds, just like before, he lifted me easily. My legs wrapped around his waist as my back leant against the wall for more stability. My cheeks grew warm under the intensity of his gaze—which somehow always felt more intimate when we were face to face, rather than in our normal height difference. "That smartass mouth is never going to go away, is it?"

"Nope."

Zack turned his head to the left to look at Theo. Like me, his back was to the elevator wall as he scrolled through his text messages. Nonetheless, feeling our stares on him, he tucked his phone into his back pocket, crossed his arms, and raised a single, questioning eyebrow. "Yes? Can I help you with something?"

I giggled and decided to poke the bear a bit more. "Yeah, you can come replace Zack and hold me instead. I don't know if he should be given attention until he cleans up. Manners, and all that."

Zack's head swiveled back my way with an exaggerated eye roll. I was half surprised that he didn't stick his tongue out at me next. "Am I going to be bullied the whole night?"

"Do you want to be?"

He hummed patiently. "I...don't know. But in case you didn't get it the first two times, I haven't had sex in eight years, so my discovery of likes is quite limited, *mi Estrella*."

Theo cut in. "I like bullying."

Zack's eyes rolled again. "Okay, no. Fuck off. Both of you."

I pouted. "Me? Fuck off? That's not very nice. If you wanted to watch me masturbate, all you had to do was ask."

On cue, they both closed their eyes wistfully, and I laughed knowing they were picturing me masturbating in unison. Both of my men were voyeurs in some form then, apparently.

I wasn't mad about it.

Theo spoke next. "That's hot. But you can fight your husband on who gets to hold and kiss you next, pretty girl. I am going to behave until I am told otherwise." Finally, after what felt like forever, the elevator let out a loud ding—informing us we had made it up to the penthouse suite.

Though, Zack stayed still as Theo stepped out of the elevator, keeping me pinned to the wall. I squinted at him questionably.

His voice was serious as he spoke and his eye contact nearly searched my soul. "You don't have to, ya know. We really can take this slow. I don't want to scare you away. I want this, yes. But I don't want to lose you again, either. Say the words, and we can just go to bed."

Was I ever going to stop fucking blushing? Probably not.

I shook my head. "I wouldn't have let either of you touch me on that Ferris wheel, in front of thousands of people essentially, if I wasn't actually comfortable with this."

"That's true. But I mean it. You don't have to jump into the deep end tonight, either."

A sigh left my throat as I wrapped my arms around his shoulders comfortably, followed by a light smile as a shiver wracked down his body once my fingers started twirling with the hairs at the nape of his neck. "You okay?"

"Yeah. Been a while since I've been touched so... comfortingly. Casually. New for me, ya know."

Oh, how I did know.

If it wasn't sex, I hadn't allowed myself to be touched in an equally long time.

My voice was thick as I gave him the reassurance we both needed. "Last night, I said the words, 'Just for tonight.' Tonight, I agreed to forever with you both. I think we've already jumped into the deep end, don't you?"

Gently, his forehead rested on mine, and I closed my eyes as I savored his warmth and the intimacy of the moment. "*Mi Estrella?*"

"Hmm?"

"You are my saint. And I am truly, utterly, your veneration."

I smiled. "This would be the time for all the booktok people to say something like, 'I am your god now. Crawl to me.' In case you wanted to know."

"What the fuck is booktok?"

Sigh. *Men.*

Or...well. Older men who were too busy to doom scroll, anyway.

"Don't worry about it."

Theo's voice pulled us apart as his head popped into the elevator doors again. "Are you guys going to stand here all night? I'm fine with elevator sex, but after a Ferris wheel, I think a bed sounds way better right about now. Don't you?"

Our heads pulled apart at his voice. "How do you know she even wants to have sex?"

His eyes locked on mine. "Do you?"

I unwrapped my legs from Zack's waist and wiggled slightly as my cue to be let down. He didn't even fight me as I slid down his tall body. "Obviously. We have a bet. I need to lock in."

"Well, c'mon then, princess."

And as Theo grabbed my hand and led me to Zack's bedroom, I could have sworn that Zack was hiding both a smile *and* a boner. I turned to him with a smirk. "Go shower. Coming in your pants is hot as fuck, but I'm not touching you again until you smell like soap."

"Oh no," I teased as Zack went to sit on the edge of the bed—my mouth nearly sore from the near mauling of Theo. He was freshly showered and wore blue and black striped pajama bottoms. My eyes traced the outline of his abdomen hungrily, just as it had of Theo's when I forced his shirt over his head. "No, no, no. I didn't say you could join us."

His head cocked to the side, forcing beads of water to drip down his chest. "What?"

Theo's hand gripped my waist hungrily as he watched Zack for his reaction, too, and I giggled as he impatiently started pulling at my shirt. I had told him to keep my clothes on until Zack came back, and I knew he was nearly gnawing the bars of his mental enclosure now. "I know exactly what I want to do tonight. Theo and I even made a game plan while you were taking care of your little mess."

Zack had never looked more confused in his life as he repeated the question again. "What? What plan? I was gone for ten minutes!"

"She wants you to watch us," Theo said, cocking his head to the side himself. He wrapped his other hand around my front so that I was firmly in his embrace, gripping my shirt tightly. "Are you okay with that?"

Zack's gaze widened as it fixed on me entirely. "Y-You want me to...watch? Watch what, exactly, *mi Estrella*?"

"I'm in the deep end, remember?" I smiled evilly. "Watch me while your brother fucks me. Be a good boy, sit in that chair over there, and watch me come on his cock before I even think about riding yours."

Theo leant down and growled in my ear. "God, that shouldn't be so hot."

Zack blinked as he stared at us both. "You want me to sit in the…cucking chair? Like, from all the hotel memes and stuff?"

I turned my head as I thought about how to respond. "Cucking is technically when I degrade you. I just told you I wanted you to watch. Consider it…a punishment, if you will. But I can degrade you too, if you'd like."

"A punishment?"

"Mmmhmm. For running out on me for your brother. Now, I'm going to fuck him first, instead of you. How's that make you feel, baby?"

He pulled at his beard roughly. I smirked, though, when my eyes travelled down the length of him and fell on the bulge tenting his pajamas. He certainly didn't look against it. "I-I don't know what to say."

I mocked him from earlier. "Yes or no?"

Theo pulled at my shirt again like an insistent child —almost stretching it—as we both watched Zack.

It was a war in his head, and he knew it.

Relinquish control enough to be in a purely submissive, vulnerable position where he had to watch another man pleasure me without touching me himself…or put his foot down and potentially disappoint us both.

Granted, I wouldn't be disappointed. If it was a boundary, I would respect that.

But it was a test all the same.

Theo grunted, and before I knew it, my shirt was being torn in half.

I gasped. "Hey! That was rude!"

"I told you that wearing this damn thing was considered cheating this morning. You should have listened to me then."

Having taken my bra off the second I laid down in bed with Theo, heat spread through my face and chest furiously as cold air forced my nipples to pebble instantly.

Asshole.

It was only a matter of seconds before I was pushed down to the bed with Theo quickly maneuvering himself to be above me. He smiled wickedly before his mouth was on my breast, sucking and biting at my flesh. The moan was practically torn from my throat as I moved my eyes to Zack again—though, he only tugged at his beard harder as he nearly growled himself.

He didn't intervene, though.

Theo released my nipple seconds later with a pop before turning his head to Zack. "What? You both needed a push. Yes or no, Zacky-poo?"

Zack didn't even act annoyed at the nickname.

Instead, he walked to the chair we had placed feet away from the bed, and sat down. Quickly, he lifted his hips up slightly and grabbed the base of his cock out of his bottoms. Theo and I both watched as he spread his legs a bit more and spit directly on it, all before he started pumping his shaft slowly.

I moaned as I watched eagerly. I liked watching him jerk off way too much. "Yeah?"

"I'll watch, but I'm joining this damn bet," he said before knocking his head to Theo. "You have until I finish. And then I'm fucking my wife, whether it's with you or without you."

i'm sorry
but i will always love you. and i'll
come back for you when i'm ready.
                              Zack

Chapter 15

ZACK

I was being fucking *cucked* by my wife and brother. *Jesus fucking Christ.*

If someone were to tell me that this would have been the direction of this entire weekend five years ago, I probably would have burst out in a fit of tears before punching a hole into the wall. Fuck, if someone told me that the events transpiring were to happen just *last week*, I equally would have laughed in their faces.

And yet, I sat in a chair, fisting my cock, as I watched my brother undress and touch the love of my life.

Unreal.

"Am I allowed to give him any direction, love?" I ground out in both pleasure and patience. "Or am I to be bullied and silent the entire duration? It's up to you."

Estrella moaned as Zack started peeling off her jeans. "I so do not care right now. There are no rules. Just be a good boy and watch me get fucked, yeah?"

My heart lurched in my throat as my dick twitched.

That was an interesting way to find out I liked being told that I was a good boy.

"Y-Yeah. Sure, okay."

Theo smirked at me. "Oh? Do we like that?"

Before I could have the chance to reply—likely to tell him to shut the fuck up and make our girl feel good—Estrella beat me to it. "Oh, shut up. You be a good boy yourself and fuck me already. I've been aching since the Ferris wheel, and I can't wait anymore."

I knew without a doubt in my mind that Theo and my complexion were the exact same. Fiery, red, and embarrassingly whiny with no warning whatsoever. Theo nodded before moving to unbutton his own jeans. "Yes, ma'am."

Estrella leaned up on her elbows to watch him strip, and I outright groaned when I saw her gulp.

I was no stranger to the size of my brother. And while that would generally be the weirdest thing someone could ever say—we lived together, and we experienced tour life together, too. I had somehow seen that man's dick more times than I had seen random girls' tits in a crowd.

Which was...a lot.

It was how I knew that her gulp absolutely wasn't faked.

"You gonna make it, *mi Estrella*?" I groaned out as my fist tightened on my length. "You gonna take that big cock while I watch?"

"I-I think he may be bigger than you. And that's... fucking terrifying. How am I supposed to take you?"

Precum dripped from my dick at her words, and as I watched Theo grab Estrella by the ankles and drag her to the edge of the bed, I was surprised that I didn't bust right then and there again.

"Move your panties to the side. I'll show you exactly how you can take me." One of his hands spread her legs while the other gripped at her waist. "C'mon now. You heard Zack. And you want to see how long I can last, yeah? Be a good girl."

I moved my hand faster. Fuck, how I wanted to blow just so I could interrupt them and be in his spot right then. "How long did she say? Ten minutes?"

"Fifteen," he grunted as he watched her move her damn panties to the side. Even from my spot on the chair, I could see how she was glistening. My mouth watered as I imagined her taste from last night, and my cock jerked once again when I thought about how she had taken my fingers so well.

Estrella chuckled. "Look at you boys. Do we need a stopwatch? Jesus. Maybe you won't even last five minutes with that kind of attitude."

I groaned. "You're bullying."

"Yeah," she hummed. "And you like it."

I absolutely fucking did.

Theo pulled her even closer and my teeth sank into my bottom lip as he dragged the tip of his cock up and down her slit before placing it right over her pelvis. "You see that? See how deep it'll be inside you? You want that?"

"Oh my God. Please. That's so...that's hot."

"Mhhm. Come here, pretty girl. What's the time, Zack?"

Jesus.

I looked at the digital clock on the nightstand. "10:12 p.m."

Chapter 16

ESTRELLA

Theo smirked above me as he rubbed the tip of his cock against my pussy, and I could have sworn that I felt a tremor pass through my legs every time that he brushed against the hood of my clit. "That means I have to last until 10:27 for our little bet. What do you say about that?"

I nearly blew him a raspberry. "*Sé hacer matemáticas, idiota.*"

One of his hands left my waist, slowly climbing until it was wrapped around my throat delicately. "Such a smart mouth. What do you say, Zack? Should we fill it to stop this never-ending attitude? Maybe we'll finally get some peace and quiet."

"At least I wouldn't be in this fucking chair anymore," Zack groaned.

I whimpered as Theo hit my clit again. I knew that I had to be leaving a wet spot on the comforter at that point. I raised my eyebrows at the man above me. "Such a dominant attitude when I'm vulnerable. Maybe I'll put you in the chair next."

He laughed, but it was quickly covered by the loud moan that tore out of my throat as I felt the tip of his dick slide into me.

Fuck. He was huge.

I obviously knew he looked huge, but looking and feeling were too completely different things.

"Yeah, baby?" Zack said from behind me. My head tipped back even more to look at him. And fuck— watching him jerk off to the sight of me, even at that odd upside down angle, had to be one of the hottest things I had ever seen. "Does he feel good? Just the tip and you're moaning like a desperate little thing."

"F-F-Fuck," Theo groaned out before I could answer. "God, she feels so good. I'm not even halfway in. What the fuck."

I moaned again as he pulled out slightly, only to push in again. "Would you hurry up?"

His eyes snapped to mine with a hint of indignation. "One day, I will ruin this damn pussy. But you have never taken me before, so be a good fucking girl and let me work it in properly. Understood?"

The snort behind me was quick to follow. "She can take it. Look at her, dripping and shaking. All that attitude until a real man fucks her, right? Maybe she should beg. Right, *mi Estrella*? You sure knew how to beg for me when you had to cum last night. Do it again."

I didn't know if I wanted to stab them or bow down to them for how they were talking about me.

Somehow, regardless of my switchy soul, I think I needed both at that moment.

"P-Please. I need you to fuck me. I need this," I begged, conceding. "I can take it. Just—please."

Theo groaned, and I watched as his eyes bounced around before his teeth sank into his bottom lip. "Don't beg. If you beg right now, I will breed this fucking pussy before you can say another word."

"*Por favor*. Please fuck me properly." My lips curled into a smile then as I reached down to wrap my hand around the leftover part of his shaft that I would still, somehow, have to take. "I need all of this in me. I'll be a good girl for you."

"You just want to win your damn bet, princess."

"Yeah, I do. But I bet your dick twitches every time I tell you ho—" My sentence was cut off as his hand slapped down on my mouth, right as he shoved the rest of his cock in me abruptly. My eyes rolled into the back of my head, and I was genuinely surprised that a scream didn't tear its way out of my throat either.

"Fuck!" Theo groaned.

I only whimpered against his hand before shifting my hips into him.

Maybe I had really bitten off more than I could chew. He was the biggest I had ever taken. It was unfair to the rest of society, and maybe even all the fictional boyfriends I had fallen in love with, too.

But fuck, I still somehow needed more.

"I know, baby. I know. I'm trying here."

Zack's chuckle mixed with his own groan. "You gonna make it, bro?"

"Fuck you."

"Thought you said that was incest?"

My eyebrows pinched together at that round of banter.

Dear God, what had I gotten myself into? I really hoped that option was not on the table. I already had enough change in life events over the last two days.

Taking back my husband and fucking his brother, for example.

Theo's hand only pressed down on my mouth harder as he began moving in and out of me slowly. My legs shook in their position, and my eyes rolled as I wrapped one of them around his waist. "Feel good, princess?"

I nodded my head, and my eyes nearly crossed as he shifted his body slightly, rubbing that spot inside of me that had me losing most of my brain cells.

A man who apparently loved me, was huge, *and* knew how to find the clit and g-spot?

I was a goner.

"That's a good girl. You feel so good to me, too. Better than I ever could have imagined."

Zack spoke behind me. "Just wait until the day we make her air-tight."

Theo's head tilted up to look at him. My moans only grew louder as he spoke and started to thrust in and out of me faster. "Air-tight? We're never sharing this girl with anyone else ever again."

"No, we aren't. But we do believe in sex toys. And our girl is greedy. I bet we could make something work."

Oh...my God.

That shouldn't have been so hot.

Something was definitely wrong with me.

My therapist was about to have an absolute field day with me.

My mother was going to behead me.

Fuck it.

"That's a true statement," Theo continued as he pumped in and out of me continuously, only to look back down at me. I already knew that I was a mess, and the drool that was seeping out of my mouth was only making that worse. He leant down to whisper in my ear. "Would you like that, princess? Being filled to the brim? To just be used as an absolute toy for us, even while we make you take one, too?"

My pussy clenching around him was enough of an answer.

Fuck yes.

"Ugh, yes. Good girl. We can do that one day."

I nodded my head as my eyes rolled. He had only increased his tempo, and I swore I had started to see stars as he kept going. I was going to finish without him even touching my clit, just from his dominance and both of them egging me on, and I didn't know if that had ever happened to me before.

Being silenced somehow sucked and was so unbelievably hot at the exact same time.

"Believe me, I'm never letting you walk away from us ever again, princess. You are ours. Our girl. Our toy. You can stay married to that man, to my brother, but it's my cock in your pussy right now. Don't forget that. You belong to us."

Fire licked up my spine.

The sound of Zack's hand slapping down on his own cock only heightened everything.

Fucking hell.

I whimpered against his hand and grabbed onto his forearm forcefully as a warning. I knew he wasn't going to let me talk until one of us had finished. He smiled down at me ruefully. "Fuck yeah. You gonna come for me, princess? You gonna try and make me lose that bet by milking it out of me?"

I tried speaking around his hand for the first time, even if it came out choked and muffled. "Please!"

His blue eyes rolled back. "Go on, then. Come for me. Come on my cock. See if you can break me."

The bet was nowhere on my mind at that point as my pussy spasmed around him. I threw my head back onto the mattress as my back arched, only to make eye contact with Zack next. His own head was thrown back, his legs spread wide, as he stroked himself to finish, too. He growled out his words. "I'll come if you do, pretty girl. I'll make a mess in my lap while he fucks you. Come on. I'm right fucking there, too. Come with me."

That was all I needed.

My eyes slammed shut as I screamed against Theo's hand.

White lightning nearly filled my vision as I spasmed around him and thrashed against the bed. It was somehow too much and not enough, all at the exact same time. And I knew without even having to open my eyes that Zack was falling over the cliff with me, based on his moans and curses.

"Jesus fucking Christ. Damn you both. I'm the only

one not allowed to come? There has to be something wrong with that rule."

My legs shook as response as he kept fucking me.

Railing me, actually.

Finally, his hand left my mouth, only to travel to my hair. I whimpered as he petted my head softly, just to grip it harder. And yet, he never stopped thrusting. "What's the time, Zack?"

Zack took a second to respond, and I tilted my head back, fighting Theo's hold on my hair in doing so. My aching moans followed in my wake as I saw him rubbing his own mess into his cock—forcing himself to stay hard. Finally, he looked at the clock, and smiled at us both. "10:30 on the dot."

Like Zack's answer was the final snap of his control, Theo's voice turned into a whimper. "Fuck it. I'm not done. I'm not done until I cum in your fucking wife. God, I want to fill her up."

"Oh my Godddd," I whined. I wanted to come again just from his words alone.

"Go on. Breed our girl. Cum in her pussy so you have lube to fuck her ass next," Zack said, and I watched as he stood up, cum smeared all over his cock, before he walked towards us. And like the feral woman I was—I only stuck my hand out for him. "You won your little bet. It's our turn to really see how much she's willing to do for us."

Everything.

I'd do everything.

"De-Deep end," I moaned out, right as Zack's fingers interlocked with mine. I squeezed roughly.

"Fuck!" Theo shouted, and I nearly cried as his hips flexed, positioning himself all the way in. I could feel him actually throbbing. "Fuck, yes! I'm coming. Take my seed, princess. Fuckkkkk."

My eyes crossed between the mixture of all three of us.

Seconds passed as Theo slumped forward, covering my sweaty body with his. Compared to his fucking, his kisses on the side of my neck were soft and sensual.

Loving, even.

His cock still twitching inside of me was way too intense of a mixture for the kisses. Overstimulated didn't even begin to describe how I was feeling, and the after-orgasm cry was probably seconds away.

At least, until it was Zack's hand moving from my hand to my hair, and tugging it forcefully enough that I cried out. Theo chuckled as he spoke.

"My turn."

700 MB
52x
80 min
CD-R
COMPACT
disc
recordable

Chapter 17

THEO

"You can't give a guy any recovery time, can you?" I muttered as I continued pressing kisses into Estrella's neck.

I couldn't tell whether I should label myself as pathetic or whipped. Probably both.

That was the best sex of my fucking life.

And of course, it was with the girl who had consumed my thoughts for over a decade.

Zack hummed out his response. "Nope. You had a bet, didn't you? Get it up, old man, or sit on the sidelines like I did. I'm fucking my wife whether it's with or without you."

Estrella whined. "What if I said I was sore? He is big, ya know."

A strong gasp flew out of her throat as her neck craned away from me again. Zack definitely pulled her hair again, and likely harder than he had before. "I would tell you that you have now made me cum twice without even properly touching me, and third time is the fucking charm."

I laughed deeply as I looked up at him. "Charming."

Though, somehow, the idea of fucking Estrella with my brother at the same time only aroused me, and I felt myself growing rock hard in seconds. Estrella moaned when I thrusted in slightly, and I moaned right along with her.

Zack spoke again. "Have you done anal, *mi Estrella*? I won't judge. Just need to know how much prep you need. I need this first time to be good for you."

"Uhm...I'm okay."

One of my eyebrows raised as I kept my eyes on her, even as my hips kept rocking. "What does that mean?"

"I've done anal."

"Congratulations. Don't be shy, though. How experienced are you with it?"

"...Very?"

I choked on my laugh, and I could have sworn that Zack's face resembled one of a downright tomato. "Very?"

"Hey! You said you wouldn't judge. And I didn't want to settle down with anyone for the risk of kids. If there were no condoms, there were clean test results and anal. Just being safe, dickheads."

I thrust inside of her more sharply that time. "Language, princess."

"*Ir a pisar una lego.*"

"Oh, you wound me."

Zack shifted slightly, bringing one of his legs down

onto the bed, and forcing his dick to be right in Estrella's face. And like the greedy girl she was, even if she denied it, she zoned in on it happily as he muttered, "Clean me off while Theo preps you."

"I'm prepping her?"

"You already had her pussy. It's my time to breed her. Do you have a problem with that?"

I shook my head as I slowly pulled out. My cock was covered in a mixture of our cum, and it took nearly all of my restraint to not wrap my fist around it and jerk off, just like that. The sight was unbelievably hot. Instead, I walked into the bathroom, grabbed the complimentary Vaseline, and immediately returned to the both of them.

Where Estrella had nearly bottomed out Zack's length in her throat.

The jealousy that hit me was nothing more than the want for her to suck us both together.

Fuck.

I laid down on the bed, watching the show in front of me for a few minutes like the absolute voyeur I was, before I called out to them, "Getting lonely over here. C'mere, princess. You're not walking away in your bratty tangents on this one."

She let Zack's dick out with a pop before turning her head to look at me. Her hair was sex crazed, and *fuck*, if I didn't want her to look like that on a daily basis. But it was her going to her hands and knees, crawling to me, that undoubtedly had my dick twitching right in front of her. "But I thought you liked my mouth."

"Mmm," I groaned before reaching for her and easily maneuvering her. I flipped her around, facing Zack, before gently pressing down on her back to make her arch more. Her ass was right in my face, and I couldn't help myself before smacking it, only to spread it apart at her moan. Reaching for the Vaseline, I immediately got to work, and I smirked as her pants filled the air.

We were both way too invested to even speak at that point.

One finger.

Two quickly after.

She whimpered as the third finger entered her ass, burying her face in the pillow. I continued thrusting them in and out slowly as Zack spoke, "What's your safe word, baby?"

"D-Drumsticks."

"Good girl. You okay?"

"Mhhmmm."

I smirked as my hand shifted, and I slowly fit in the fourth finger. Her moan at the addition was loud and guttural, and yet, her hips only shifted backwards for more.

God damn, was I whipped for that girl.

I finally broke my own silence as my other hand moved to circle her clit, forcing her to moan loudly again. "I think you're ready for us, baby. All prepped and needy. Tell me you're ready though."

"I-I'm ready."

I turned my gaze to Zack. Ever so slowly, I pulled my fingers out of her, only to grab her by the waist and drag us both back. Every inch of her was red from a mixture of arousal and humiliation, and fuck, I was disappointed I didn't have a camera to capture it.

Next time.

Finally, a deep grunt fell out of my lips as she laid flat against me. I wrapped one arm around her torso as Zack lifted her hips up slightly—enough for me to insert the tip of my cock—and my mouth dropped open as she slowly sank down on me.

"Fuuuuuck," she moaned out, gripping at my arm around her forcefully. "You're so big. Holy shit."

I grunted as she sank down another few inches. "You can take it. You're doing so, so good for me."

She whimpered, and in moments, her ass was fully seated with my cock inside of her. I leaned my head back as Zack spread her legs even wider, taking in a deep breath. He nudged the head of his cock at her entrance, still dripping with my cum, and bit my lip as he spoke. "I'm not going to go easy, baby. I need to breed my girl. You said you wanted kids earlier, didn't you? This is us giving you what you want. That okay with you?"

"Just fuck me already, dammit."

I laughed, only to groan when he thrust in deeply.

Estrella's head flew back onto my shoulder, and I used my other hand to gather and grip her hair as Zack thrust in and out again. "Fuck! You couldn't have been gentle on the first one?"

I tugged Estrella's hair myself that time. Her eyes flit to me as her mouth popped up on Zack's next thrust. He groaned loudly, and my dick twitched at the feeling of him rubbing against me through her walls. It should not have felt that fucking good. "Are you complaining?"

She cried out on his third thrust, and her legs shifted even wider herself. Any more and she would probably be doing a split. "N-No. Fuck, it's so good. It hurts, but it hurts so good. Don't stop."

I craned my neck down to kiss her forehead, only to shift my own legs slightly. "Good girl. Take these two big cocks. We'll blow so hard in you like this. I bet you wanna take both of our cum, don't you?"

"Fuck!" Zack groaned, thrusting harder.

"Yes!" she moaned out. "I need it. Don't go slow. Just give it to me. I can take it."

Zack looked away from her and onto me. "You heard our girl. Fuck her, too. C'mon. Let's ruin her for anyone else."

"Oh my God," I ground out, teeth clenched. I listened to the both of them, though, and moved my hands to her waist, gripping roughly before thrusting up into her myself. As Zack pulled out, I thrust in, and we equally fucked her in full strokes continuously. She was a chaotic mess of babbling moans, and I knew I wasn't going to last nearly as long as I did the first time. Heat was already spreading through me.

I spoke again. "Who do you belong to, princess?"

Her answer held no hesitation. "You!"

I watched as Zack leant down and rubbed two fingers on her clit in fast, tight circles. "Just him?"

"N-No! Both of you. I belong to both of you."

"Good girl."

"Fuuuck," I ground out again. My balls needed to be emptied right then. "Fuck, I'm gonna come. I'm gonna cum in this tight little ass. You want it, baby?"

"Yes! Oh my God, I'm gonna come. Come with me!"

And like a fucking ticking time bomb, I could have

sworn we all grew tight and frantic at once. Zack and I changed our thrusts to match each other's, forcing her to be as tight as possible. She shifted with us, eager. My hand that had been holding her hair traveled down to her tits, and the second I pinched and tugged at one, her back was bowing against me.

"Oh my God, oh my God, oh my God!" she screamed.

Zack thrusted in sharply one more time, bottoming out entirely, as he came with her, grunting. And as I felt his own dick pulsing right through her, my own head was thrown back on the pillow as cum spurted out of my dick, filling her entirely. An endless sea of wrecked pleasure and filth. We both pulsed and shook for nearly an entire minute, and by the time it faded, exhaustion wracked me entirely. Estrella's body had gone limp, laying on me, and I took comfort in the weight and fullness of her, even if it was unbelievably dirty and sinful.

Her hand pushed against my abdomen lightly and I groaned. "I'm dead. I think I died. I'll never recover."

Zack chuckled as he gained his composure, too. He leant down, leaving a soft, loving kiss on her mouth, before slowly pulling out. Estrella and I both sagged at the relief and lack of fullness all at once. "We're right there with you, baby. We gotta get you cleaned up now though, okay? Then we can all die."

I sighed. "Yeah. C'mon, baby. Let me shift you off slowly. Then we can all shower and get some sleep."

She nodded as a yawn tore through her. "You're both sleeping with me."

My hands squeezed her waist, forcing her to squirm. "No shit. We just did it."

That time, it was Zack who rolled his eyes. "She meant sleep, sleep. Snoring, sleep. Dumbass."

"I mean...both work do work though, yeah."

And as a laugh ripped through my chest, I somehow had never felt so warm.

i'm sorry
but i will always love you. And i'll
come back for you when i'm ready.
                              Zack

Chapter 18

ZACK

My hand flew out to the side of the mattress where I knew Estrella would be, and I groaned as I found it cold. Not a trace of warmth was in the mattress. My eyes remained shut as I moved my other arm out, thinking she had probably switched sides. Only, I frowned when I found it equally as cold.

My eyes cracked open, and I grunted as sunlight hit my vision immediately. After blinking a few times, I glanced at the clock and cursed. 11:11 a.m.

The time to make a wish.

I wished my wife was still in fucking bed with me. Even my brother would have been a comfort after last night.

My brother...

Jesus, I was going to rot in the absolute depths of hell.

But man, was it absolutely worth it to have the love of my life back in my life.

Sighing, I tossed the comforter off me and walked over to the suitcase. In seconds, my boxers were on, and I walked out into the living room space of the suite. Only, I nearly tripped over myself as I saw Theo sitting at the kitchen counter with his head in his hands, shoulders tense, staring down at something.

"What's going on?" I asked, and he jumped. Any other time, I would have given him shit for the way he spooked so easily, but something felt wrong.

And where the fuck was Estrella?

He only shook his head.

I walked towards him and peeked over his shoulder. Right in his hands was a napkin with, undoubtedly, Estrella's handwriting. I grabbed it from him without a second thought and read the words, smeared after being touched by Theo so many times, and my heart dropped into my stomach.

I'M SORRY
IT WAS TOO MUCH. TOO SOON.
I'LL ALWAYS LOVE YOU TOO. BOTH OF YOU

ESTRELLA

Theo sniffled as he wiped at his nose with the back of his hand. It was only then that I realized he had been crying. "We fucked up, man."

I reread the words over and over again. As if there was any other meaning in the words.

As if I hadn't done this exact same thing to her years ago.

I somehow wanted to tear the napkin in half, yet hug it to my chest at the same time.

Theo continued again, and his shoulders shook. "She's gone. I asked the hotel staff if they had seen a girl with green hair leave this morning. They said yes."

No.

No, no, no.

Fuck no.

I slammed the napkin on the countertop and stormed back into the room. In seconds, in both fury and panic, I had reached the side of the bed where my phone was on the charger and went to dial our media manager. If worse came to worse, I would be the asshole in the situation and pull the, *our photographer dipped out on us, where is she* card.

A low blow.

But I meant it when I said I was never letting this girl go again.

Except, as I scrolled through my text messages to find her contact information, I stopped short at a group chat at the very top of my texts labeled "Heart Attack Helpline" with a picture of Theo's contact info in it, too.

I clicked on it with a furrowed brow.

UNKNOWN NUMBER

> Bet I scared you, didn't I? Payback is a bitch.

> Alas, I have not run away from you brooding men. I just have morning plans with the drummer of Obsidian Static. AND I have to buy a new shirt since SOMEONE ripped mine.

> I'll see you at your show tonight <3
>
> PS: I am sore as fuck. One of you is
> giving me a back massage tonight.

"Theo!" I yelled, even as I found myself smiling down at my phone. "Check your phone, dumbass!"

As I typed up my response, I heard his footsteps nearly running to his own bedroom.

ME

> You gave us a heart attack.

I changed her contact name in my phone right as my phone buzzed, telling me she had already responded.

ESTRELLA

> Duh. Why do you think I labeled this
> group chat the way I did?
>
> Gotta keep you old men on your toes.

THEO

> I've been crying, princess.
>
> I thought you left.
>
> You're coming back?

ESTRELLA

> Obviously. If I wanted to ghost you, I
> would do a better job than this.
>
> International.....SUPERSPYYYYY

I burst out into laughter as Theo walked back into the room shaking his head.

She hadn't left.

We would be okay.

I typed out my own response before tossing my phone on the bed.

ME

We deserved that.

You're still being punished later for this stunt though. Maybe. Maybe I really am just the asshole.

See you tonight, pretty girl.

"Estrella!" I called out as I saw a flash of black and green hair jogging towards our security tent. She stopped dead in her tracks at the sound of my voice and turned around slowly. "Can I talk to you for a second?"

I had been debating the course of action and how I wanted to give her something for hours at that point, and I was sure that one of the guys was about to behead me. Especially as I kept droning on and on during our practice round of the additional song.

I needed to rip the Band-Aid off.

I couldn't help but feel like I was about to propose again though.

She walked towards me until she was in ear shot. "Am I in trouble?"

Theo, who stood at my back, chimed in, "Yes."

"Then, no."

I rolled my eyes as I shoved Theo. "We'll talk about

your little stunt this morning later. We deserved it though, so no, you're not in trouble. I just wanted to give you something before the set starts."

Her eyebrows squeezed together in confusion. "You're giving me gifts? Why?"

"Because you're my wife?"

Theo snorted before tapping my shoulder sympathetically. "Good one."

Her eyes bounced between the two of us. "I'm confused."

I only shook my head as I took out the small envelope out of my back pocket.

The envelope that I had brought with me to every single concert for years. As a good luck token.

As a...what if?

But a gift she had sent me herself, along with another round of divorce papers, years ago.

"It's technically not a gift if it's already yours," I said before handing it over to her. She took it gently before peeking inside, and it was mere seconds later before her lip started to wobble and tears filled her eyes. "You don't have to wear it. I know...we're all a package deal now. So, I will understand. But you're still my wife. So, if you do want to wear it, it's yours."

She took the wedding ring out of the envelope slowly.

Her wedding ring. Encrusted with obsidian diamonds in a silver band, in the shape of her star-sign constellation.

Theo spoke slowly as she gazed at it, wiping away

her tears. "If you do decide to wear it, I have dibs on getting you a fat diamond for your other hand. It's only fair."

Estrella burst out in a fit of tearful giggles. She looked at me as she spoke though. "You mean it?"

I nodded before slinging my arm across Theo's shoulder. "Deep end, baby girl. Till death do us part. Told you I was never signing those damn divorce papers."

"Yo!" We heard a voice shout behind us, and I craned my neck to see Elijah, Alex, and Tyler staring at us with a mix of disgust and happiness. Disgust...somehow behind the main emotion.

The dickheads.

Tyler droned on. "We kinda have a thousand people waiting on us. Can y'all continue this later or something? Emotions are weird and I am uncomfortable."

Theo shook his head as he headed towards them, but not before he pressed a kiss to the top of Estrella's head. "Thank you for staying."

She hummed her response.

I snaked my arms around her next. "We'll see you out there. We're even playing you a song."

Her head quirked to the side at that as she fiddled with her wedding ring. She slid it onto her left-handed ring finger smoothly. Right where it belonged. "Oh? What's it called? I didn't know you all had any new music."

I smiled before leaning down, grabbing her hand, and placing a kiss on her wrist. I stared right at the ring as I spoke, deciding to give my attention to the day and time period that started it all. "Contrition. I think you'll like it."

THE END.

Acknowledgments

To Tilly, first and foremost, because... wow, my mania really said, "Hey... hey, let's go bug your best friend into writing a shared world..." and we *actually* did the damn thing. While I want to say that this will be the last time I convince you into slightly irresponsible decisions—we all know that is certainly not the case.

To Hannah at English Proper Editing Services, who is truly my go-to girl—thanks for taking all my chaos and filth with stride, and for making me feel confident about my words when doubt creeps in. Sorry for almost making you throw your laptop on this one though <3

To Bria, who continues to help me grow every day, and without her, I'd be a flailing fish in the sea.

To my ride or dies—Katie, Eli & Sierra—who support me through the thick and thin. I love you weirdos.

And lastly, to T—my best friend and bestest supporter. You're not even shocked about the storylines I throw at you at this point, and I love that. Thanks for reminding me to take breaks and drink water when all I want to do is hyper-fixate though. My yellow heart, always. <3

Want More

FROM C. S. SILVERNE

While many ideas are constantly brewing, feel free to check out
the following titles for more in the C. S. Silverne world <3

Preyless: An MMF Military Romance Novella

Clueless: An MMF Forbidden Romance Novella

Longing for More: A Forbidden Military MFM Novella

Contrition: A Second Chance MFM Rockstar Romance

Prideful Ache: An Age Gap Romance Novella

CO-WRITES WITH TILLY RIDGE:

Play The Game: A Dark Masked Why Choose Romance Novella

Ride the Line: An MMF Forbidden Romance

Run the Night: An FFM Age Gap Romance

Birdie: A Small Town Sapphic Romance

About
C. S. SILVERNE

C. S. Silverne is a twenty-something year old author who spends a lot of her time hiding behind a computer as the true introvert she is—between writing words, designing pretty pictures, reading her kindle, or blaring the latest rock music release—it's guaranteed she's trying to ignore the world in some emo fashion.

Even in her forbidden and occasionally taboo writing styles... she takes light of her pseudonym, always finding love in the silver linings of the world. Because, as we all know, sometimes—love chooses us in the strangest, cruelest of ways, and the stories of the forbidden deserved to be told.